SHOWDOWN

The two natural enemies measured each other bleakly. Fire flew from their crossed glances and the outlaw leader's leathery face slowly grew mottled.

Palmer stiffened. A deep, bitter dread of Helm Spink had always plagued him, motivating his extravagant attempts to insure that Spink never came back to the Roost. Everything had failed, and here was the sorry result.

In the yellow light of the hanging coal oil lamp there was a flashing blur of movement. Spink rolled his Colt up simultaneously with the apparent clumsiness and lightning swiftness of a grizzly's striking paw.

Gunfire blasted thunderously . . .

Other Avon Books by
Peter Field

DIG THE SPURS DEEP
GUNS FOR GRIZZLY FLAT
GUNS ROARING WEST
RIDE FOR TRINIDAD!
WAR IN THE PAINTED BUTTES

Coming Soon

COUGAR CANYON
OUTLAW DEPUTY
RAWHIDE RIDER

Avon Books are available at special quantity discounts for bulk purchases for sales promotions, premiums, fund raising or educational use. Special books, or book excerpts, can also be created to fit specific needs.

For details write or telephone the office of the Director of Special Markets, Avon Books, Dept. FP, 105 Madison Avenue, New York, New York 10016, 212-481-5653.

A POWDER VALLEY WESTERN

MAN FROM ROBBER'S ROOST

PETER FIELD

AVON BOOKS • NEW YORK

AVON BOOKS
A division of
The Hearst Corporation
105 Madison Avenue
New York, New York 10016

Copyright © 1957 by Jefferson House, Inc.; copyright renewed in 1985 by Peter Field (pseudonym for L.W. Emerson)
Published by arrangement with Thayer Hobson & Company
Library of Congress Catalog Card Number: 88-92106
ISBN: 0-380-70425-0

All rights reserved, which includes the right to reproduce this book or portions thereof in any form whatsoever except as provided by the U.S. Copyright Law. For information address Thayer Hobson & Company, P.O. Box 430, Southport, Connecticut 06490.

First Avon Books Printing: January 1989

AVON TRADEMARK REG. U.S. PAT. OFF. AND IN OTHER COUNTRIES, MARCA REGISTRADA, HECHO EN U.S.A.

Printed in the U.S.A.

K-R   10 9 8 7 6 5 4 3 2 1

1.

HAZY SEPTEMBER SUNSHINE lay over the brushy swells of Powder Valley, tucked snugly under the eastern rim of the lofty Culebra range in southern Colorado. Bee-buzzing languor had burned away the early morning crispness which spoke of advancing fall. It was a blazing diamond of a day.

Four men rode from the mouth of a wild and winding canyon gashing the Culebra flanks. By their looks they had laboriously and warily crossed the ragged range, disregarding the beaten trails and at some cost to both clothes and horseflesh.

Jack Gentry, youngest, hardiest, and most cheerful of the four, pushed his jaded mount to the crest of a grassy rise from which there was a wide view over the slumberous valley. Helm Spink, a burly and grizzled giant of coolly dominating manner, rode up to join him. Together they gazed out over the quiet rangeland, hunger and hope in their eyes.

"This is just the right country to winter in—if we can pick up jobs and ain't recognized," Spink spoke up gruffly.

Jack Gentry nodded ready agreement. "It'll help if we're not all seen together right at first. We haven't been spotted yet . . . That'll be Dutch Springs yonder." He pointed to the distant blur of the little cow town toward the center of the valley, barely visible across the dun-colored swells.

"Yeah." Spink digested the information before turning to wave the other men forward. He waited till they were close. "We'll split up here, boys," he announced flatly. "That's town over there—and we better drift in an hour or so apart. That'll make it look accidental enough."

Fred Sparks and Trap Hagen nodded. Middle-aged and rough-looking, more accustomed to life on the open range than in towns, neither was much given to words. "We meetin' again there, or what?" Hagen asked uneasily.

It was Gentry who answered. "There's a back-alley livery. Garford's, or some such thing. We can lay our plans there after we look Dutch Springs over. Nobody'll notice that."

They assented briefly. "Meet yuh there, then."

After another word or two between Spink and Gentry, the four separated, each melting into a brushy fold. Jack Gentry was in no particular hurry. He rode north alone, following the natural cover till he came out on the Ganado trail. With easy assurance he turned into it and jogged toward Dutch Springs.

Reaching town shortly after midday, he racked his bronc and turned into a hash house. He ate leisurely, like a man with nothing on his mind. But he was careful not to miss any face, and it was a private relief when he spotted no one he recognized.

As he strolled down the town's one street afterward, Gentry watched Fred Sparks ride into town past him without a sign. Spink and Hagen would be showing up presently. Jack was passing the hotel, glancing across at the Gold Eagle saloon opposite, when he suddenly froze. A small, gray-haired man, who limped badly as he worked, was listlessly sweeping the porch over there. He was obviously the swamper, and he did not so much as raise his eyes from the warped boards underfoot. Gentry never took his sharp glance off the slight figure till the man finished his task and stumped inside.

Gentry loitered before the hotel, making a show of preoccupation. A moment later, however, he strode quickly across to the corner of the Gold Eagle, glanced this way and that to make sure he was not observed, then slipped down the side of the building to its rear.

As he expected, the swamper was making a pass or two

MAN FROM ROBBER'S ROOST

at the back steps with the broom. The old man looked up absently as Gentry made directly for him.

"Limpy! You old son-of-a-gun," was the young fellow's warm greeting, delivered in a carefully lowered voice. "What in creation are you doing here?"

The swamper flushed, his watery gaze faltering. "Well, it's a livin', anyhow." He waved indifferently toward the saloon. "Pretty far off the reservation yourself, ain't you, Gentry?" There was a defensive note in his voice. It would have been hard to say if he welcomed this unexpected encounter.

Jack hugely enjoyed his own silent laugh. "Slack off, old-timer," he chuckled. "I know what you're thinking. But this visit is strictly on the level . . . Come to think of it," he added, his tone solemn, "there's some friends of yours in town. I know you'll be glad to see them." He named Helm Spink and the others, narrowly watching the effect of his news.

Limpy's features hardened as he listened. "I don't like it. You and Spink ain't up to no good," he muttered dourly.

"No—we're fed up with the owl trail," declared Gentry earnestly. "That's gospel, Limp. We're thinkin' about getting jobs." Jack talked on in his smoothly persuasive manner. He had long since become known as an oily-tongued diplomat, a fact with which the swamper was perfectly familiar.

Limpy fidgeted with the broom undecidedly, finally laying it aside. "Where is the bunch now?" he muttered.

Gentry mentioned the livery, and the thin little man started that way without ceremony, through the backyards. A moment later Garford's barn came into sight. Helm Spink and Sparks were standing in the big door, eyeing Gentry and his companion.

"If it ain't Limpy Parsons!" Spink rumbled. "Dang it, I've been askin' myself what became of you—"

Trap Hagen rode round the corner just then. Glimpsing Limpy, he gave an exclamation. "Well, blast my buttons!" He was frankly amazed. "What is this—Old Home Week?"

Limpy squinted at them with no softening of his manner. "The pack of yuh are up to some high jinks," he accused harshly.

"Sorry to disappoint yuh, Limp." Hagen was grinning through black-bristled jaws as he dismounted. "We're lookin' for honest work. Can yuh tie that?"

Limpy snorted. "You'll all go to work," he predicted cynically. "When you're about as stove up as I am, and not before. That's if you're around that long!"

Spink's lazy contempt made it obvious he didn't care what the swamper thought. "If you're safe around here, Limpy, there's a good chance for us . . . Of course, you look different nowadays!" he added callously.

They fell to discussing in low tones their chances of employment in Powder Valley. Limpy, however, refused to treat their pretensions seriously, though Gentry indulgently probed him concerning the sizable ranches in the valley. They were still talking when a rider jogged past the mouth of the alley leading in to the barn from the street. The stranger was a broad-shouldered, keen-faced individual, and he appeared to be a capable rancher as well.

Gentry broke off what he was saying, turning to Limpy at once. "Who is that?" he asked quickly.

"Pat Stevens." The swamper made a disposing gesture. "Forget about him, Jack—"

"Has he got a spread?" Gentry urgently interrupted.

Limpy's nod was grudging. "Lazy Mare, up the valley." He was reluctant to add more. Gentry didn't wait for anything else.

"Come on. Introduce me," Jack proposed, taking the shrinking swamper by the arm and trying to force him forward.

To his surprise, Limpy flatly refused. "Unh-uh! Nothin' doin'. Leave Stevens alone, Gentry. He's poison, I'm tellin' yuh!"

"So for argument's sake, he's lightning with the bark on. What of it? I can still work for him, can't I?"

Limpy was not to be beguiled. "Yuh can steal from him too—once," he retorted bluntly. "Don't try to tell me yuh plan on anything else!" Not too many years back the swamper had been one of them. Sheer age and incapacity, rather than conscience, had persuaded him to go straight at the last, though his imaginations still rode with the wild bunch. He was convinced now that he understood thoroughly how the minds of these four worked. "When things go wrong—and they sure will—just forget that I ever laid eyes on yuh. I don't want to know nothing; I won't lift a finger to help—and that's final!"

Gentry glanced expressively at Helm Spink, then shrugged. "Sit tight," he advised, turning away, "and I'll see what I can do."

Limpy sputtered behind him as he strode out to the street, but Jack paid no heed. He had taken shrewd note of Pat Stevens's roan mount in the bare moment at his disposal, and now he spotted the animal at once, tied at a rack down the street.

Walking that way, Gentry scanned the store building before which the horse had been fastened. *JEB WINTERS*, the weathered sign read. *Groceries. Gen'l Merchandise. Post Office.* Jack stepped in confidently. The Lazy Mare owner was here, talking to a stout, aproned figure who could only be Winters himself. Gentry waited till a pause fell in their conversation, then stepped up to the merchant.

"Winters, I expect?"

Jeb nodded, swiftly taking the other's measure. "That's me. What can I do for you, neighbor?"

Jack's response was offhand. "You hear the news. You might know of a rancher or two looking for hands." He made sure the words were clearly audible.

Winters's glance sharpened. "Don't belong on this ranch, do yuh?"

Gentry shook his head. "Just riding through, looking for any cow work that offers—"

Pat Stevens, who had been attentively following this exchange, moved forward. "Excuse it, Jeb . . . Did you say you're looking for work?" he asked Gentry.

"That's right." Jack looked interested. "I can sure use a job, mister."

Pat nodded. "You look healthy. Know how to handle stock, I judge. You can go to work right off, if my offer suits." It was roundup time, with help scarce; and he was not disposed to be too choosy. He named his terms, a shade above average for this range. Gentry promptly stuck out his hand.

"I'll shake on that. What brand am I riding for, anyhow?"

"Lazy Mare—a few miles north," Stevens introduced himself, and Gentry followed suit directly, watching sharply for any unfavorable reaction. There was none.

"Fine, Jack." Pat was practical. "I can sure use you. Roundup's on—the fact is, I could handle half-a-dozen men to good advantage."

Gentry had counted himself lucky to catch on so handily; but this was unprecedented good fortune. He hesitated. "Since you put it that way, Stevens. I was talking to a grub-liner just now down at the livery—"

Pat agreed readily to the implied proposal. "Find him, then. I'll talk to him."

Carefully concealing his elation, Jack walked rapidly back to Garford's barn. Spink and the others saw him coming. They awaited his opening words with curiosity. "Did yuh make the riffle?" Hagen demanded eagerly.

Gentry nodded, grinning. "Nothing to it. I found jobs for us all—on the same outfit." He met their incredulous looks triumphantly.

Fred Sparks snorted. "That ain't smart, Jack," he protested strongly. "I thought we wasn't even supposed t' know each other!"

Gentry's grin broadened. "Look. This Stevens is hiring help," he explained. "I'm helpful. I mention running into a grub-liner—and Stevens says go get him. So I find three instead of one. Simple, isn't it? I never saw you birds before. We get acquainted gradual, like any new hands on a spread—and that's it."

They signified their comprehension, though Spink was the last to give his approval. "You got a fast way about you," he grumbled. "But this looks all right—from here."

Jack was impatient with their hardheaded caution. "I'll take you to Stevens, and you can do your own talking," he snapped.

"Just don't forget I warned you birds," Limpy called after, as they trooped out of the alley at Gentry's heels.

There was a grizzled, hard-bitten cowman talking to Stevens when they arrived before Winters's General Store. "Zeke Johnson—my foreman," Pat introduced him tersely.

"Howdy, Johnson," Jack waved to the wary trio behind him. "Look what I run into. I don't know these hombres," he qualified, turning to Stevens. "But you said you could use more help—"

Pat indicated with a nod that he was willing to let Johnson handle the situation. The foreman had already taken shrewd measure of the four. He bit out a question or two, concentrating on Helm Spink, and seemed to linger over his decision.

"Kind o' queer, four of yuh turnin' up in a bunch," he growled.

"What's funny about it?" Spink met him bluntly. "I want work—and I come where work is."

"Same here," Hagen seconded, and Sparks merely nodded.

"All right." Johnson made up his mind quickly. "The four of yuh can ride out to the Lazy Mare with me."

"Well, hold on." Pat turned to the new hands. "Zeke and I are closing a stock deal here in town. The four of you better stick around for an hour or two, and we'll all go together. Satisfactory?"

They chorused their gruff assent, careful to turn away in different directions. Johnson, the Lazy Mare foreman, had already judged them critically, and it would not do to give him food for further unfavorable thought. Ten minutes later, by devious routes they gathered once more at Garford's.

"We got our jobs," Helm Spink commented with a trace of grimness. "And that ramrod ain't going to be too easy to please. Any of yuh don't like this setup, now's the time to pull out." He scrutinized their faces.

Hagen scoffed. "This'll be a sour pill, boss. But we'll play it straight." He paused then. "Yuh don't reckon old Limpy will blow on us—?"

Gentry promptly derided this fear. "He don't much like

our showing up here. But he's every bit as worried as we could be. He'll keep his mouth shut."

They could only hope he was right. Talking the situation over desultorily, they concluded themselves fairly safe in Powder Valley for the present. From now on the future must dictate its own course.

"Don't any of yuh forget there's a chance we could be trailed out of the Roost even now," reminded Helm Spink curtly. "I don't think that's anything we can't handle—but keep your eyes open, just in case."

They were to remember his words before the day was over. At Gentry's suggestion they presently split up to avoid comment or observation, waiting for the call from their new employer. Pat's deal must have presented delays, for the afternoon waned without his putting in an appearance. Shortly before dusk Johnson located Spink.

"Find the others and get your supper at the hotel," he directed. "Tell them to charge it to the ranch. Afterward you can meet me down at the public corral, and we'll be ready to shove off."

Helm Spink was a big man, enormously sober and not overly articulate. He only nodded and moved off to find his companions. They ate at a corner table in the hotel dining room, and once finished, left without delay to get up their mounts. Dusk was thickening now, but they saw Johnson waiting before the wooden gate in the high corral fence at the upper end of town.

"Let's see. We're all here, I reckon?" The foreman counted noses as they gathered about him. "Guess we're not missin' anything except Stevens—"

The words were scarcely out of his mouth when the flat, spiteful crack of a gun rang out. It seemed to come from between a couple of sheds in the brushy lot across the street.

Before anyone could speak or move, Zeke Johnson uttered a muffled groan and started to slip out of his saddle. Gentry was barely in time to catch him, while Spink hastily dismounted and ran to help ease the unconscious foreman to the ground.

Hagen and Fred Sparks whipped out their Colts and sent

several hot slugs whining into the shadows. Not content with that, they rammed their horses into the brush around the sheds.

There was no more firing, but Pat Stevens came running up the street almost at once. "What was that about?" he demanded harshly.

Spink rose and turned. "Dunno, Stevens." He was gruff. "Some hombre fired on us while we was waitin' here. He got Johnson. The boys went after him—but I reckon he's gone now, or they'd have drilled him by this time!"

2.

PAT HAD NO EYES for anything but his foreman. "What's he laying there in the dust for? Pick him up, hang it! We'll get him into the hotel or somewheres."

Genuine concern sharpened his voice as he bent to help lift Johnson from the ground. Together he and Gentry got the wounded man partially erect. Stevens was preparing to hoist him over his broad shoulder when the foreman sighed and started to move feebly.

"Hold on. He's comin' to—" Spink snapped a match and held it up. "Why, there ain't nothing wrong with him but a nasty graze on the head!"

Fred Sparks returned just then, his gun in his hand, muttering to himself. "That ornery skunk got clean away," he cried out disgustedly. He started to add more, but Spink cut him off brusquely.

"Bring a drink from the nearest bar, you. Get moving!" he barked.

Sparks hurried off on his errand. Before he was back, Johnson was once more in full possession of his faculties. The whisky made him shudder, jolting him wholly awake.

"That was a gunshot! Some wolf tried to pot me—" Zeke's crusty indignation suffered a check. "Oh-h, what an achin' head." He touched it gingerly.

"Can you navigate, Zeke? . . . Better step up and let Jeb Winters slap some salve and a bandage on that crease. You're all over blood." Masking his solicitude, Pat satisfied himself that Johnson could make it and urged him on his way. Then he turned back to face the new hands.

All four were gathered again and waiting with dour

expectation. "Well, Hagen," Pat rapped curtly. "Did you find out anything?"

Trap's grunt was expressive. "About as much as Sparks here. I heard the shot—it came from around them sheds. But that hombre was awful quick on his legs, Stevens. And it's gettin' dark fast—"

Pat made no effort to inquire further into their investigations. He looked the four over critically. "Which one of you," he asked suddenly, "has got that kind of an enemy?"

Their pause was marked. Then everyone tried to speak at once. "Hell, not me!" Trap Hagen declared vehemently. "What are yuh drivin' at, Stevens?" Spink seconded blankly. Jack Gentry attempted to speak for them all. "I reckon none of us was looking for that kind of a surprise," he ventured, a note of puzzlement in his voice. "It don't make sense."

Pat quizzed them sharply for a moment or two without any satisfaction. "You might as well come clean if you know anything," he pointed out. "I back my outfit. But I like to know what I'm up against."

They remained stubbornly silent. It was Gentry who began glancing up the street from moment to moment. "Wonder how Johnson's making out. There wouldn't be anyone laying for him that you know of, Stevens?"

Pat's disclaimer was terse. "Better go after him though, Gentry. I'm anxious to get him in his bunk. If he can ride, we'll shove on out to the spread."

Jack turned away at once. The uneasiness with which the others waited, and the interest they displayed in Gentry's speedy return, told Stevens much. It was obvious that they were anxious to leave town as quickly as possible.

Johnson appeared presently with Gentry. He had regained his normal poise, and with it more than his usual share of curtness. "Why not shove along with these fellers," he suggested to his employer. "I'll be along in the morning—"

Pat chuckled. "No—I know how you feel. But you'll come now, Zeke. You can use some rest," he reminded dryly.

The grizzled foreman proved unexpectedly balky. "What's

the objection, Stevens—so long as I do my work?" he demanded.

"Dutch Springs isn't our bailiwick, for one thing. And there's no sure proof that attack was anything but accidental. Tell the sheriff your story, if you insist, and let it go at that."

"Okay. Skip it." Johnson had no interest whatever in the local law enforcement officer. "We gettin' started for home, or what?"

The new hands revealed their readiness by pushing their broncs forward. Johnson swung astride his waiting mount, and with him and Stevens in the lead, they set off for the Lazy Mare. Night had fallen. They soon left the lights of town behind and jogged through the cool, starshot darkness.

Johnson's wound had taken more out of him than he would admit, though he thrust on doggedly. Pat took advantage of his grumpy silence to drop back for a word with one or two of the newly hired punchers. Observing Gentry's persistent effort to draw him apart from the others, Stevens let him manage it, curious to learn the reason.

Jack did not leave him long in suspense. "Stevens, there's something I think you ought to know."

"What's that?"

"Why, I overheard the boys talking after that ruckus. Sparks and Hagen seemed to guess pretty well who did that shootin' . . . It could be a flare-up from something or other on their back trail. Spink got it too. I seen him looking at me queer." Gentry spoke urgently, at the same time pretending uncertainty. "Johnson won't thank us for bringing anything like this to the Lazy Mare—or you either. It seemed like my job to warn you."

"Thanks. I'll keep it in mind." Pat's nod was brief. "What, exactly, did you overhear, Gentry?"

Jack now seemed reluctant. "I guess it's fair to judge that pair have got an enemy," he said finally. "No names mentioned—but one they know about only too well, whoever he is. I even seemed to gather," he hinted darkly, "that Johnson was mistaken for you. It was dusky, you know—"

"Just what gave you that idea?"

"As you say, it's largely a notion," Jack hastened to

confess. "Hagen and Sparks caught us listening and shut up."

There was more talk on the subject, though no new information was added. Stevens did not mention the matter to the others—he had his own ideas about Gentry's motive. Jack's story somehow established too patly the lack of connection between the four men, although Pat realized that every one of them was concealing something.

What this might be was of minor importance beside the fact that Pat needed punchers. He had long depended on his own ability to handle his crew, and it was no different now.

Stevens was still concerned about Johnson, when they reached the Lazy Mare an hour after dusk. "Better let Crusty Hodge have a look at that head, and then pile in your blankets right away," he advised the foreman as they drew up at the corrals. "Spink—look after Zeke's bronc, will you?"

Johnson snorted, dismounting. "Old Crusty needs his own head examined," he growled. "I'll be all right. And I can take care of my own horse!"

Pat would have objected, but his attention was distracted as the door of the ranch house kitchen clattered open and a raucous voice sang out.

"Where in time yuh been, Stevens?" It was pudgy Sam Sloan who waddled officiously across the yard, a snaggle-toothed grin splitting his blue-bristled jowls. "We been hangin' around an hour waitin' for yuh to show up—"

With him was Ezra, a horse-faced and red-headed giant with a single shrewd eye. He was Sam's partner in the little Bar ES horse ranch down the valley. "It's a wonder yuh wouldn't stay home once in a while," he rumbled in his bass voice.

Gentry and Spink stiffened to attention at the approach of this pair, looking them over sharply in the dim light. Ezra and Sam returned the compliment with cool effrontery when they spotted the strangers. Sloan in particular eyed them critically, in the manner of a man buying a horse.

"Company, huh?" he huffed, "From the looks, I must say yuh ain't very particular—"

Pat began to laugh at his frank disapproval. "Oh come, Sam," he protested mildly. "What would you say their opinion was of you if it depended on looks?"

It was true enough that even in this rough country few men presented a more disreputable appearance than Sloan and his long-legged companion. Though coarse and offensive of speech as a rule, the pair were far from prepossessing and seemed deliberately to cultivate their piratical aspect. It did not alter the fact that they were friends of long years standing, warmly valued by the younger man. Both knew this and took canny advantage of it.

"Well—there's your own handsome puss to be considered while we're on the subject," retorted Ezra with sour emphasis. "They can't amount t' much in the first place, hirin' out to a hombre like you."

Ignoring this, Pat briefly introduced Spink and the others. "It's roundup time for us unfortunate stock raisers—and I need help. I was lucky enough to pick up these boys in town," he finished in a faintly admonishing tone.

"Call it luck if yuh want," demurred Sam dubiously. "I take it you're payin' these birds a salary?"

Pat was puzzled. "I usually do—"

"Wait till yuh get your money's worth and then crow," the little man advised. "If yuh don't get something else along with it, then yuh will be lucky."

Gentry listened to this plain talk with a frown. "Just who are these hombres, Stevens?" he began angrily, staring at Sam.

Pat waved the challenge aside. "Friends of mine, Jack. Maybe it'll help if I say their bark is worse than their bite—"

Waiting for no more, Gentry and his companions turned abruptly in the direction of the bunkhouse. Pat stood watching till they were beyond earshot before he turned again to the crusty partners.

"Neither one of you went out of your way to make those boys welcome," he observed carefully. "What have you got against them, anyhow?"

The lanky redhead shrugged. "If we had anything, Stevens, you'd hear it—and them too," he returned bluntly.

"It ain't anything yuh can put a finger on. I just don't like their looks, is all."

"Yes—and if you're smart yuh won't take your eyes off 'em for longer'n it takes to sneeze," seconded Sam earnestly. "I know yuh won't pay no mind. Yuh never do. But just don't forget we warned yuh!"

"You'll remind me if I'm in any danger of forgetting." Pat shrugged the matter off there.

The talk turned to other things, and it was late when the outspoken pair set out for home. For all that, Stevens was astir with the crew the following morning. One of his first chores was to make sure that Johnson was fit for a day's work. He found the foreman in the bunk room, already up and stalling off the solicitous attentions of Jack Gentry.

"How's that head this morning?" Pat queried directly. "Okay, is it?"

"You too?" Johnson was gruff. "Don't be fussin' over me! Big day comin' up, Stevens, and I ain't got time for no such claptrap."

Pat concluded from this that the man was once more his usual competent self. At the same time his concern for the foreman's welfare gave him an excuse to work with Johnson's crew today. It was no accident that Zeke also planned to take Helm Spink and the other new hands with him. He wanted to see what they were made of.

They were working the west range, where the Lazy Mare graze bordered on wasteland and the empty hills. It meant hard riding, chousing the strays down out of the draws and second-growth timber. Pat was prepared to put in a day like any other puncher; but he managed also to keep a sharp eye on the drifters.

Not greatly to his surprise, they were all first-rate cowmen. They seemed to vie with one another in clattering recklessly over the roughest ground, and not so much as a single steer escaped their vigilance. Not one was a shirker. They did their work with zest, and it was not long before they began to earn approving glances from the regular hands.

"Dunno where you picked them boys up, Stevens. But they're all right," grizzled Eph Sample found occasion to remark. Sample was himself a one-time derelict whom Pat had picked up and give a chance. Old and gnarled as he was, Eph had made good.

Pat nodded. "They'll do to take along—if they keep up the pace they're hitting now," he made the cagey reservation. He had run into whirlwinds before, only to watch them slow down with passing time.

"That's true. You ain't always around," commented Eph shrewdly. "And Johnson is watchin' them fellers like a hawk just now—"

Pat suppressed a grin. "What would you take from that, for instance?" he asked.

"Zeke figures they ain't altogether innocent in that mysterious shootin' no matter what they say. I think the same myself. Not that that's anything against 'em—but there's no harm in knowin' what you're stackin' up against."

It was another plain warning for Pat to watch his step where these strange men were concerned. He said no more, but he did a certain amount of thinking; and he was instantly alert when, early in the afternoon, the Lazy Mare punchers began calling to one another and gesturing toward the south.

Stevens could see little at the moment from where he was. But he noted the banner of dust rising into the sky a mile or two south. This could mean only a moving body of stock, and for a second he was unable to account for it. The Lazy Mare gather was not being held in that quarter— nor did he know of any cattle that might be moving there. It was a situation that required looking into.

Dropping his place in the line, Pat rode down the willow-bordered arroyo, scrambled up its far edge and made for a swell which afforded clear sight across the tumbled range. The dust thickened off to the south, marking a sizable herd. He still could not see too well, although the cries of the Lazy Mare hands came from the distance. He rode that way and gradually converged with several of his men, all as keenly curious as himself.

"Somebody movin' a big bunch across your range, Stevens," Trap Hagen called. "They're workin' west. Didn't know there was a spread off that way—"

Pat was thinking rapidly. "Could be somebody's bought

McDonogh's little Spade range in Coldwater Canyon. Jock folded a season or two back, and it's been lying idle."

The traveling herd, which must have numbered nearly a hundred and fifty head, was spread out raggedly—and that spelled either a careless drover or a short-handed crew. They pushed close enough to read the brand.

"Circle C Bar," Jack Gentry sang out. "Where's that from, boss?"

Pat shook his head. "Don't recognize it. Probably from the plains country over east."

"Maybe that young feller can tell yuh something," suggested Helm Spink, pointing.

A lithe figure on a paint pony drifted into sight along the flank of the herd. But when Stevens whistled and the face turned toward them sharply, they saw that it was a girl. She spotted them. Instead of riding to join them, however, she raked her horse to a mended pace and passed on, soon becoming obscured in the enveloping dust.

"Huh! That's kind of queer," remarked Hagen suspiciously. "They tryin' to cover up, or what?"

Pat thought not. "Just busy." He believed he knew now why the stock was straggling along so loosely. It was in charge of such a small crew that they found it impossible to do better.

A minute later Gentry pointed silently at another driver. Pat was astonished to see a middle-aged, stocky woman, stone-faced and with iron-gray hair, hazing the stock along with raucous cries. Like the girl, she noticed Pat and his men and waved a casual greeting without bothering to turn her mount.

"Well now, if this ain't something," Gentry was grinning broadly. "Petticoat ranch, and no mistake about it!"

Pat was growing more interested by the minute, though he said little. He was keen to learn what was going on and was about to jog out to accost that burly female. But Hagen's next words arrested the impulse.

"Here comes a young cow prod bringin' up the drag," Trap exclaimed. "He'll be able to tell us the sad story . . . Say! Something familiar about him, too—"

As he spoke, he pushed forward to intercept the oncoming puncher. Pat let him go, awaiting the result with interest. Hagen jogged close to the young fellow. Suddenly he stiffened. To Pat's amazement, he struck the puncher headlong off his horse and leaped down to drag the other violently forward. A dozen feet from Stevens, he whirled the astonished man around.

"I don't know who this is, Stevens—never seen him before," Hagen burst out harshly. "All the same, this is the rat that fired on Johnson in town last night! There can't be no mistake about it!"

3.

PAT STEPPED DOWN out of the saddle to confront the young puncher. "Who would you be?" he asked gravely.

"Tell this devil to turn me loose!" Struggle as he would, the puncher could not break Hagen's iron grip. "What's it all about, anyhow?" he panted. "I never saw you before—or him either!"

"Did you do that wild shooting in town last night?" Pat demanded flatly.

"Shucks no! What shootin'?"

The puncher was vehemently in earnest. Stevens made a sign to Trap, who let go and stepped back a foot. The other, a dark-haired young man with lean, ruddy face and crackling blue eyes, stared about, nursing his wrenched arm. He glared resentfully at the gathered Lazy Mare men.

He never had time to vent his injured feelings. The stocky woman had seen enough to persuade her to abandon the stock long enough to straighten this hitch out. She barged forward now with a considerable show of impatience.

"Now what?" she blurted belligerently, her forbidding underlip thrust out. "What are you good-for-nothing men interfering with my help for? Speak up!"

The big woman straddled her heavy work horse competently, and she acted and looked much like a man. Pat decided it was largely her bulldog jaw and blazing dark eyes that contributed to her masculine air.

"Just who are you, ma'am," Pat's question was respectful but firm.

"Pickett's the name. Or Madge if I happen to like yuh." For all her brashness, she knew how to be circumspect under pressure. "I bought out Jock McDonogh over here in the mouth of Coldwater Canyon, mister, and I'm moving the stock onto my new range." Her bushy brows lifted shrewdly. "This a sample of the welcome we can expect in Powder Valley?"

"Pat Stevens, Mrs. Pickett. You're crossing my Lazy Mare spread. Some of my boys were fired on in Dutch Springs last night. Your—puncher seems to be mixed up in it, unfortunately."

"Who—Kip Colerain? Pah! Nonsense!"

"Well, he was!" Trap Hagen burst out hotly. "He did it, because I saw him!"

"You saw me in town, you mean. What does that amount to?" young Colerain snapped angrily. "I was already hired out to the Picketts. And you're no part of my work!"

"Hold on now, boys." Madge Pickett intervened authoritatively. "Let's get to the bottom of this before my stock scatters to hell and gone." She eyed Pat accusingly. "Do I understand you're backing this preposterous charge, Stevens?"

"I'm inquiring into it." Pat was blunt. At the same time he began to entertain a real respect for this self-reliant woman. She was doing no more than vigorously backing up her hired help, as he would have done in like circumstances. "Colerain *was* in Dutch Springs last night, I take it?"

The answer came reluctantly. "Ye-es—"

"And what's more, I was paying strict attention to my own business," young Kip exclaimed. "How come this Nosey Parker saw so much of me? If I'd fired at him I wouldn't have missed!"

"Why you mouthy punk—!" Hagen was about to leap fiercely at Colerain when Jack Gentry grabbed him by the arm and whirled him around. Trap glared at him momentarily. "What's the idea?" he bellowed.

Gentry released him, at the same time coolly shouldering him back. "Just don't lose your head, old boy," he advised. "*I* was there last night—and I didn't see this fellow. Why not tell us what makes you so sure of yourself?"

MAN FROM ROBBER'S ROOST

"Humph! There's one man with a mite of sense anyway," Madge Pickett snorted. Pat overheard her comment and could not help wondering if this was the effect Gentry was cunningly striving for.

"Dang it, don't tell me what I saw!" Hagen exploded. "There must be some reason why you're protecting this blasted sharpshooter—!"

They wrangled briefly; and Gentry clearly did not intend to be overridden. But Trap persisted heatedly. "Well, if you're so sure this fresh kid wasn't there, let him tell us what he was doing," he exclaimed truculently.

Though he'd been on the point of shutting them both up, Stevens thought this last proposal a reasonable one. "Maybe you can supply the answer to that, Mrs. Pickett." He turned politely to the burly woman.

She appeared inclined to go just so far in her efforts toward conciliation. "I don't try to keep track of everybody—least of all for the likes of him!" She indicated Hagen contemptuously. "Let him prove Kip was throwing lead around, if he knows how. It's his claim."

The words nearly precipitated another angry clash. Before it got started, however, a feminine voice spoke up calmly. "Perhaps I can help you there."

It was the girl who had previously ignored them to ride on with the stock. None had noted her return till she came close to face them. Clearly she had screwed up her courage to the point of entering this argument, and her dark eyes were snapping. Pat found it easy to admire her quiet spunk.

"I don't believe I've had the pleasure, Miss—" he hinted, with a twitch at the corners of his mouth.

"She's India, my daughter," Mrs. Pickett interposed.

There could be no mistaking the strong family likeness between the two women; but that was as far as it went. The girl was slim and feminine, and her impact on these hard-bitten men could not be missed.

"Then you know what Colerain was doing last night—is that what you mean?" Pat continued with no change in his gravity.

"I do." She could put on dignity when she chose. "He was helping me all evening. I was buying supplies."

Hagen glared at her. "Are yuh swearin' to that, girl?" he demanded hoarsely.

Her eyes widened without a trace of fear. "I certainly wouldn't say so if it weren't true." Her calm innocence of tone effectively defeated the rough-mannered puncher.

Pat grasped this opportunity to clinch the matter. "Then that settles it, of course. You must have mistaken Colerain for somebody else," he told Trap blandly. "Our apologies, Mrs. Pickett. Naturally we have to look into any such affair pretty close."

Madge Pickett sniffed. "Kind of late to be explaining yourself, seems to me. But I expect I can look forward to more of the same. I've run into quarrelsome outfits before."

Pat smoothed a rueful smile off his mouth. "No, I think I can promise we won't give you any more trouble, ma'am. In fact, I'll see to that myself. I aim to be neighborly. If there's any way I can help you, let me know."

Although he caught an approving response in India Pickett's eyes, the girl's hard-headed mother only grunted. "It was no favor holding us up while my stock scatters over all creation," she grumbled spitefully.

"I know—sorry." Pat spoke quickly. "Let me give you a couple of men to help finish the drive."

"No. I've made it this far, Stevens. I'll make it the rest of the way—barring any more interruptions." Mrs. Pickett turned to Colerain and her daughter. "Well! Are we waiting for something?"

In awkward silence the Lazy Mare men watched the trio jog after the scattered herd. Trap Hagen alone looked stubbornly resentful and as though he half expected a reprimand. Pat could not help noting also the lingering look Jack Gentry sent after that slim, erect girl.

The Picketts were soon busily hazing their stock together, and they presently disappeared over the swells. Pat turned his horse, putting a firm end to the episode. "All right, boys. There's work waiting for us."

He made no further mention of the affair, although he was aware that it was being discussed at odd moments by the others. The new hands continued their display of energy, and by late afternoon that entire section of the range had been thoroughly worked. The results were above expectation, and Stevens was well pleased. While a minor loss of stock from predators was inevitable, it promised to be a prosperous season. Even Johnson was cheerful that night in camp.

"Wasn't no mistake pickin' up those hands in Dutch Springs," he remarked to Pat. "We'll fill our usual commitments, with beef to spare."

"Thanks mainly to you," the Lazy Mare owner assented.

Johnson shunted away from such compliments in a hurry. "I hear we got neighbors over west," he changed the subject gruffly.

Pat told about Mrs. Pickett's having bought out old McDonogh in Coldwater Canyon, mentioning the encounter that afternoon with the little Circle C Bar herd. "They won't give us any trouble, being that far up in the hills," he predicted. "I'm glad to see Jock's old range occupied—not that I don't think the old girl will have her troubles. Jock always did."

The foreman appeared to have something else on his mind, however. "What's this about her puncher being the hombre that let fly at me?" he demanded finally, a chill glint in his eye.

"Nothing to it," Pat assured him lightly. "I don't know that fellow from Adam. But it's plain Hagen was being hasty. He made a mistake, Zeke. I'd swear to it."

Johnson's nod was dubious. "I'll take your word for it. All the same, this Hagen bird'll work for his keep. I'll turn him and the others loose tomorrow on Iron Ridge."

The area he mentioned was a lofty and barren spine composed mainly of weathered rock, lying roughly between the outermost fringes of Lazy Mare range and the country around Coldwater Canyon. Despite the almost complete absence of water, outlaw steers loved to hide in the tortured draws and rough breaks of the forbidding ridge.

There was just enough light the following morning for Johnson to point out Iron Ridge to Helm Spink and his fellows before the quartet jogged away to their day's work. The chore was more than calculated to keep them busy, but the giant range man seemed well content to be turned loose on his own responsibility, and he took charge of the little crew with firm competence.

Pat watched their preparations for departure with quiet interest. "I don't know what you'll find over there," he remarked to Gentry. "But make a clean sweep—and don't miss any of those rocky hollows. The mosshorns have been taking to that country in droves, and the gather could surprise us all."

"Leave it to us, boss," Spink broke in heartily. "We'll herd the grasshoppers out of them rocks if yuh say so!"

Watching them ride away, Pat spent a moment's sober thought on the big man. If he spoke at all, Spink was always ready with an easy jest; and he seemed cooly determined that things should go right. He had remained conspicuously in the background during the clash with Kip Colerain the day before, but it was plain that he could play a decisive part when he wished. Stevens concluded he was well worth keeping an eye on.

Pat put in a hard day on his own account, with the results continuing to prove more than satisfactory. As he returned that night to the roundup camp he could not deny a certain curiosity about the report expected from the new hands. To his surprise the four had not yet put in an appearance, although dusk was already thickening on the open range.

The rest of the Lazy Mare crew, who had been working nearer at hand, had long since arrived. Belcher, the camp cook, had fed most of them. He was snarling at the rest, urging them to get it over with so that he could wash up, when a clatter of horses sounded, and the belated punchers rode tiredly into camp.

They were all long-faced and silent. In the campfire's flickering light Pat saw that their horses were unusually gaunted, denoting hard and rough travel. Obviously they had put in a rigorous day. He stepped forward with narrowed eyes.

"What luck, Spink?" he asked their acknowledged leader.

Helm shook his bushy head. "Poor, Stevens. Mighty poor. Wasn't a dozen head t' be found on that damned stone pile. We shoved 'em all down—but I kind of thought there'd be more." He looked faintly baffled and disgusted. "Sorry, but that's the story."

"A dozen head!" Zeke Johnson shoved close, staring at

the weary riders. "Hell, man, there's got to be ten times that many on Iron Ridge! There always was. Are you dead sure you worked that ground real careful?"

"We worked like dogs, Johnson," Gentry replied with dogged resignation. "What Spink tells you is true. The stuff just wasn't there."

He had more to say, and Pat heard him out quietly. It could be true. Yet, although the count on Iron Ridge did not matter greatly, it seemed queer. An extended discussion was broken up by Belcher's belligerent threat to throw the rest of the supper out.

Spink and his silent companions ate. Afterward they showed a complete willingness to talk over their unfruitful day. They were still batting the topic around an hour later, with some of the regular punchers already turning in, when Eph Sample stood up at the fire, listening.

"Somebody comin'," he announced tersely.

After a moment the approaching horse could be heard more plainly. It did not escape Stevens in the interim that Gentry and Spink both backed unobtrusively out of the direct light of the fire.

A man rode directly forward and reined up within a dozen feet. "That you, Stevens? Thought I'd find you here," came the gruff words. It was Rufe Dade, the lanky Powder County deputy sheriff. He turned his cadaverous face toward the men gathered about the fire. Pat was civil, though he had never liked the man.

"What brings you here, Dade?"

"Rustlers," the deputy growled. "A big, tough female named Pickett moved onto Jock McDonogh's place yesterday, Stevens . . . Didn't take the thieves long to strike. They got away with a good fifty to sixty head of her Circle C Bar stuff last night or this mornin'."

Pat stood up at the unpleasant news. "Why, we haven't had any rustling around here for quite a while," he exclaimed. "Maybe a head or two killed for beef, but nothing worse. Are you sure of this, Dade?"

Rufe's look was glowering. "I'm sure that stock is gone," he insisted sourly. "I reckon it didn't fly—"

"Any idea who did it?" demanded Pat, ignoring the sarcasm.

"Yes. I have." The answer was as decided as it was unexpected. "And what's more, I aim to lay hands on the guilty parties in short order!" Dade dismounted as he spoke, his movements deliberate. The men in the camp waited in tense silence for what was to come next.

"All right—speak up!" Pat was sharp. "Who are they?"

Rufe slowly scanned the close faces, then pointed a blunt forefinger. "Him—and him—and him." To no one's great surprise he indicated Helm Spink, Gentry, and Trap Hagen. Probably the omission of Sparks was accidental, for the man had faded from sight moments ago.

"I see." Pat spoke levelly. "What makes you pick those particular men out, Dade? They were seen, no doubt—"

"No. But who else is new on this range, Stevens? What's more, I've seen them hombre's faces before somewheres—on a wanted dodger, likely!"

It took the accused trio a second or two to realize the gravity of the charge being leveled at them. Jack Gentry was the first to speak up.

"Hold on there, mister! You've got us dead wrong," he declared hardily. "Don't try to pin a rap like that on us because we happen to be new around here! This Pickett woman is new too, if it comes to that! We're working for Stevens here. Not a one of us laid rope on that Circle C Bar stuff, or whatever it was. I know, because we were together all day!"

The deputy measured him contemptuously before turning back to Pat. "What about it, Stevens? Maybe you can give a satisfactory account of their activities—since you were foolish enough to hire 'em."

Pat hesitated. If the accused men had done what they were told today, they were in the clear. At the same time he was perfectly aware that, with their gaunted horses and the meager results of their gather at Iron Ridge, it was entirely possible the new hands could have been industriously rustling Mrs. Pickett's herd instead of doing their duly assigned work. They had the motive in Hagen's frankly revealed enmity toward Kip Colerain—and they could have made the time, for all the result produced by their riding. At the least, it certainly looked bad.

4.

"You heard them say they're Lazy Mare hands," Pat told the deputy coldly. "You're not laying a hand on them now, Dade, no matter what you think."

Finding that Stevens meant to back them up with something more than words, Spink and Jack Gentry quickly regained their aplomb. Hagen went so far as to leer at the lawman triumphantly. Rufe put on a scandalized look, glaring at Pat.

"Yuh must know how far you'll get by taking that line," he yelled angrily. "That's obstruction of justice, pure and simple, Stevens, and nothing else!"

"Oh, no." Pat lost nothing of his coolness. "Far from it, my friend. I intend to look into this business myself, starting tomorrow morning. You can wait—or you can leave now. Suit yourself!"

It suited the deputy to cling tenaciously to his original flimsy contention. "Then I'm stayin'," he declared stubbornly. "I never could see goin' back to tell Sheriff Lawlor that Pat Stevens sent me home, and I won't start now!"

Pat had no more to say, and he turned his back on the other. Thereafter the entire camp gave Rufe the cold treatment. Another man would have taken the hint and withdrawn to a respectable distance; but Dade had always been thick-skinned. He hung on, muttering to himself. He finally rolled up in his blankets in the very midst of the crew.

He was still there in the early dawn, already up and watching everything about him with suspicious eyes. Pat was by no means the last to roll out, for he was concerned about the unlucky Picketts. Breakfast was eaten in silence,

Rufe Dade partaking with the others. When they were ready to start Stevens turned to his foreman.

"I'll be taking the new hands today," he informed Johnson quietly. "No reason why this should halt our regular work. We'll get back as fast as we can make it."

Zeke only nodded, making no reference to Fred Sparks, who had been on night herd and was now snugly asleep in his blankets, oblivious of the early morning bustle about him. Dade was mounted and waiting when Pat and the others got ready to pull away. He jogged up beside Stevens officiously.

"What's your plan, Stevens?" he demanded importantly as they set off.

Pat's sidewise glance was cool. "We'll be doing what you should have done, mister—picking up the trail of that stolen stock. And we'll stick to it."

Rufe seemed impervious to barbed thrusts. "Fair enough. And I don't want any of you other birds trying to pull out on the sly," he said glowering offensively at the three.

"Don't worry." Gentry had long since had more than enough of Dade's effrontery. "A little more of your blab, chum, and we'll chase you all over the rocks. You won't be able to get rid of us!"

Dade snorted. Not quick-witted enough to be intimidated by this chilly brand of talk, he contented himself with a further display of his overbearing manner. Pat ignored the byplay, striking straight for Coldwater Canyon.

Jock McDonogh's little spread lay in the wide mouth of the canyon. The ranch house was a tight cabin of jack-pine logs, situated on a bench beside a mountain creek which tumbled down out of the Culebras. A tangle of corrals stood off at one side. The ranch had long been called the Spade, from the shape of the lower canyon. The part of the range which lay outside the canyon was by no means all of it—good graze extended for some distance up the canyon proper; and Stevens soon determined that on her arrival Mrs. Pickett had probably thrown the Circle C Bar stock into the protection of its walls.

"We'll stop at the house first," he announced briefly.

Madge Pickett saw them coming and barged out into the yard with a fighting look. "Now what?" she bellowed. "Come to tell me you didn't have no luck?"

"No, ma'am. Haven't tried yet. But I intend to." Pat noted that her flannel shirt was scrupulously clean this morning, and though she was big it was good sense for her to wear Levis around a working ranch. "I wanted to ask what you know about that stolen stock."

"I know it was stolen." Madge was tart. "I hope you don't question that, Stevens!"

Pat, however, was not to be browbeaten. A grin tugged at his jaws. "*I* don't know a thing beyond what I've heard, Mrs. Pickett. But my men have been accused, and I expect to find out the answer. Maybe you can tell me which way the rustlers went."

She stared a moment before waving up the canyon. "Good grief, man! It's your guess. I drove the stock in here—it's gone now. You must know this range better than me!"

Pat heard her out soberly. "Then as near as you know they didn't come down past the ranch—"

"No, they didn't. I don't sleep that heavy, I hope!"

"That's all I need. It shouldn't be impossible to trace fifty or sixty head in the canyon. We'll give it a try anyhow."

Trap Hagen had been scowling at the woman, doubtless expecting a tirade. As Pat and the others turned away, he stared about the ranch yard warily. "Where's that wild kid puncher?" he growled. "I hope he ain't primed to cut loose at us again soon as our backs are turned!"

Madge withered him with a look of scorn. "G'wan. You ain't nothing to brag about yourself, from your performance."

Hagen would have retorted, but Helm Spink quickly silenced him. Rufe Dade covered the touchy moment by speaking up in his officious way. "Don't worry, ma'am. Reckon I got the guilty hombres tabbed—and we'll have them beeves back too, if it's humanly possible."

"Lot o' good that'll do you," Trap put in savagely.

"You ain't hardly human . . . Accuse a man of rustlin' and then expect him to help you find the stolen stock!"

"All right. Let's get down to business here," Pat interrupted impatiently, and this silenced them. They rode up the long canyon, missing nothing, and it was still early when the remnants of the pillaged Circle C Bar herd came into view. Spink pressed on past, sticking close to Pat, his experienced eye studying the ground underfoot. Gentry was similarly occupied.

"Here's the sign of a sizable bunch," he called out, presently. "It worked straight up the canyon."

Their pace quickened when they saw that he was right. Coldwater Canyon wound back into the rising hills by means of a devious course, and the character of the ground changed from time to time. More than once they struck rocky going where they saw no prints whatever. Each time the trail was picked up farther along, but Pat knew enough about this country to gather that sooner or later the tracks might peter out for good.

This happened even sooner than anticipated. In its upper reaches Coldwater was intersected by a number of branches, through several of which the rustled stock might easily have been driven. However, the hurried drive seemed to have passed them by when the sign abruptly faded out on stony hardpan a hundred yards short of the point where the canyon split into two main forks.

They shoved on, hoping to pick up the hoofprints again. But the steers seemed to have disappeared into thin air for all the trace that remained. The five hauled in at the forks, glancing about the craggy, pine-cluttered ramparts. They had already climbed to a comparatively high level. From here the branch of the canyon that wound off toward the south looked grassy and well-watered. The other led up into the heights, narrow, rocky and denuded, a far from enticing prospect.

Rufe Dade took one cursory look upwards and turned toward the other fork. Pat watched him forge on for a dozen yards, then called out to him. "Where you going now, Dade?" he demanded irritably.

"That stock must've been drove this way, Stevens,"

Rufe called over his shoulder in a superior tone, without turning back. Jack Gentry glanced at Spink and shrugged. They were no more inclined to follow the deputy's lead than Pat was. Rufe caught on with a rush and came pounding back, his face a thundercloud.

"Tryin' to give me trouble while I'm locatin' that stock, are yuh?"

"Not a bit of it," Pat retorted. "Shove right ahead, Dade. I aim to investigate this other branch before I go any farther." There could be no mistaking his calm decision, yet Rufe chose to argue.

"Blast it, nobody'd drive steers into that rocky hole unless he had a hole in his head! You're just wasting my time, Stevens!"

"I'm wasting my own—if that's what you call it. I told you to go ahead, if you insist."

Dade cursed under his breath. "I can spare ten minutes, I suppose, since you aim to be bullheaded about this," he conceded sourly. "All the same it's plumb lost motion. You'll see."

They pushed on, soon finding themselves in a narrow, pinched defile. It did seem rather unlikely that cattle had ever been deliberately driven this way. For all they knew, this fork might prove impassible at any point. Still it wound on, craggy and silent. They were forced to be careful of the horses' legs as they doggedly followed its course.

It was Spink who drew up a few yards in the lead to wait for Stevens. At Pat's approach the big man silently pointed down at the ground. The Lazy Mare owner was scarcely surprised to see the fresh droppings there. He called to Dade, indicating the evidence without comment.

Rufe's homely face turned ugly. "Huh! Given' yourselves away, are yuh?" was the only thing he could think of to say. The suggestion was so patently preposterous that no one bothered to retort.

Farther along, the rocky branch canyon grew broken and incredibly fissured. Its crumbling walls were castellated, and side vents and tributary gaps opened out on every hand. Pat insisted on exploring them all, at least after a fashion. Despite Dade's bitter complaints at the waste of effort, this course finally paid off. They came at length to a hole in the stone bastions that led to a green pocket tucked away in the maze of granite.

Gentry started to push in there, then hauled up to stare in amazement. He let out a whoop. "You're a smart one, Stevens! Here the stuff is, sure enough—without the loss of a single head, from the looks!"

They all crowded forward to have a look. The whole story was plain. Since they had no inducement to stray from the feed in this secluded cache, the Circle C Bar steers were all where they had been turned loose a few hours ago. They were untended. Not a soul was about.

Rufe Dade scanned the situation, then whirled. "Well! This is your finish, Spink," he announced heavily. "You and Gentry and Hagen signed your own tickets by leavin' the stock here!"

The three went stony of face. Jack alone found words, as he eyed the lawman narrowly. "How do you make that out?"

"Simple! The three of yuh was workin' Iron Ridge yesterday, alone—a matter of five miles from here. I learned from Johnson that yuh didn't bother to bring in no Lazy Mare stuff to speak of. Good reason why! Yuh were all busy somewhere else." He glared at them condemningly. "Yuh can consider yourselves under arrest for this barefaced deal!"

He spoke with finality; and indeed his plausible reasoning seemed to settle the matter. As he was being disarmed, Spink visibly fought down the impulse to violence, appealing to Stevens with a helpless look.

Pat shrugged, though he realized the other's anger, "You'll admit yourself it looks bad," he murmered. "There's not a thing to justify my blocking his play. But take it easy. This affair isn't over yet. Won't be, till Dade slaps you all in the jug."

The long-faced punchers were of two minds how to take the situation. An arrest for rustling was usually a nominal charge since it was virtually impossible to prove guilt, and circumstantial evidence had never yet been made to stick. None of the three would have greatly minded a night or two in jail, provided it would end there. Not one of them, however, could be certain he would not be recognized and as promptly charged with far more serious crimes. Moreover they all felt decidedly ill at ease minus their guns.

"We drivin' Miz Pickett's critters back down the canyon?" Hagen demanded. Well aware that the operation might take hours, the crusty rawhide cunningly hoped for an opportunity to slip away and disappear.

Dade quickly disillusioned him. "Leave the stuff be," he ruled. "They ain't going nowheres for a while. You are."

The three exchanged forlorn looks. Stevens followed their thoughts accurately enough. They all were fully capable of disposing summarily of the deputy; but they were not yet prepared to go that far. He spoke up decisively to end the uneasy truce.

"We might as well get on back to the Lazy Mare," he said. "Maybe we can thrash this tangle out."

"You'll supply a guard to help land these bad apples in the calaboose, Stevens," retorted Dade flatly. "That's how we'll thrash it out, and don't make no mistake about it!"

No more was said as they turned back down the canyon. Only Rufe was in a hurry, and he prodded them along unmercifully. It was close to midday when they drew near the Lazy Mare roundup camp from which they had started. Pat's regular crew was waiting for word of their success, and it did not take long for Candy Evans to worm out of Dade the true status of affairs. The other hands promptly bristled at this cool arrest of three of their fellows, regardless of how new they were.

"We'll take them boys away from Dade in a hurry, boss, if yuh say the word," Eph Sample offered gruffly.

Pat promptly vetoed this. "We won't make any mistake here. Right now we'll shove on over to the ranch, boys," he announced, "I'll see that Spink and the others get all the breaks they've got coming."

Cryptic as this remark sounded, it quieted the grumbling crew. After a hasty bite, Pat and Rufe Dade shoved on with the captives, the deputy growling because Stevens had thus far refused him an extra guard. It did him no good since Pat cheerfully ignored his barbed remarks.

Early in the afternoon the Lazy Mare headquarters buildings came in view. Pat's glance sharpened as he noted several saddled broncs in the yard. He recognized a couple of them and was not surprised when Sam Sloan swaggered out of the bunkhouse.

"Danged if I ever found yuh home yet," the latter tossed at Pat insultingly. "Don't know why I even expect it any more—"

Pat favored him with a level look. "Suppose you explain your own trespassing."

Sam nodded, grinning. "I can do that fast." Turning back to the bunkhouse, he gave a gruff call. "Ez! Trot them trained wolves out here—"

Dade and the three punchers followed this exchange with faint astonishment; and none were prepared for it when the tall redhead appeared, jostling two bound and glowering prisoners into the open. Pat was alert in a twinkling.

"Where did you pick up those handsome gents?" he demanded sharply.

"Caught 'em runnin' off that Pickett woman's cows," informed Ezra proudly. There was a triumphant glint in his single shrewd eye. "We seen the whole thing, Stevens, while we was over there nosin' around, and we grabbed 'em while the grabbin' was good. What's more, I can tell yuh right where them stolen steers are if yuh want t' know. What's wrong with that?"

It was obvious from the brightening faces of Gentry and his companions that there was nothing whatever wrong with it. Pat turned at once to the flabbergasted deputy.

"There you are, Dade. Signed, sealed, and delivered. It only goes to show how easy it is for a man to make a mistake once in a while, don't it?"

"Hold on. I ain't so sure of that!" Rufe bristled angrily. He whirled on Sam. "You saw so much, Sloan—how sure are yuh them stock thieves didn't have some helpers? Say about three, if we're comin' down to cases!"

Spink and Hagen began to mutter angrily at this new observation. Dade's meaning could hardly be misunderstood; but Sam only returned the deputy's bitter look blankly.

"Why, no. If there'd been more of 'em, Dade, we'd have grabbed 'em while we were about it. Where'd yuh get such a crazy notion?"

This was plain enough. Yet Pat caught the blistering glances now being exchanged between his new hands and the guilty prisoners. He had little doubt that these men knew one another only too well. And it was just as certain that questioning them about it would do no good whatever.

5.

"ALL RIGHT—COME OUT WITH IT! What's the verdict, mister deputy?" Gentry demanded loudly, ending Rufe's stupefaction.

"Reckon I'll have to let yuh go this time," allowed Dade lamely, shaking his head as though he had suffered a personal loss. From his sour expression he didn't relish the taste a bit.

Helm Spink laughed harshly. "Big favor," he jeered, "Why, you horse-faced lunkhead, you're plumb lucky we don't demand an apology!"

It would not have taken much more to make Dade boil over, had he considered himself on safe ground. As matters stood, he was content to take Sam and Ezra's prisoners in charge and start immediately for Dutch Springs. Sloan consented to accompany him, determined to lodge the guilty pair safely in jail.

"I expect Miz Pickett ought t' be notified about her stock," remarked Ezra as soon as they were gone.

"Yeah—that's right," Spink spoke up promptly, following developments with interest. "Jack and me'll go along, Ezra, if you're goin' over there."

Ez was about to protest this arrangement, and he glanced toward Pat. But for once Stevens was indifferent to his likes or dislikes. "You've got that much coming to you after being accused of lifting those steers," he told Spink reasonably. "Tell Mrs. Pickett I said you and Gentry can help drive the stuff back on her range. If she can use you for a part of the day, that's all right."

36

Both men caught at this with ill-concealed eagerness. "Much obliged, boss. We ain't above doing the old girl a favor . . . Let's go, Ezra!"

The lanky man shook his head. "If you're goin', I won't have to," he growled. "I ain't no hand at dealing with women anyhow. They make me nervous."

Pat greeted this solemn pronouncement with a burst of laughter. "I'd like to see something bother you—outside of that partner of yours," he jested. "He makes even me nervous!"

Ezra loved nothing so much as a hot dispute with Sam, but he would allow no one else to attack this squat man. "Dang you, Stevens!" he blared. "He's a better man than you are, right now!"

There were all the makings here for a fine hassle, but Spink and Gentry did not wait to hear it. Swinging astride once more, they set out on the double for Coldwater Canyon. Though they talked over their recent close call, they did not slacken their pace much until the Spade range came into view.

"We'll have to see the old lady, I suppose," Gentry observed as they neared the Pickett ranch house.

Spink stole a glance at his face. "So what's wrong with that? You're figuring to shine up to that girl, ain't you?"

Jack grinned candidly. "We understand each other," was his light response.

They pounded into the yard a moment later. Madge Pickett thrust her head out of the door, giving them a distrustful look. "You two?" She came rolling out in an apron which looked somehow incongruous on her.

"Good news, Madge—Mrs. Pickett, I mean." Spink affably appeared to have lost all his diffidence. "Your stock's been located, and that deputy's got the crooks in tow. He's takin' 'em in to town now. We figured you'd be glad to know."

"I am." Madge's face cleared and her manner relaxed slightly. She paused then. "You—wouldn't be pulling my leg now?"

"Shucks, no! I wouldn't do that, ma'am." Spink grinned unabashed. He proceeded to recount briefly the events of the morning. "That Dade made a mistake about us, but he knows better now," he proceeded. "Stevens asked us t' help yuh get your cows back."

"Now, that's fine." She beamed on him circumspectly. "Kip's up the canyon somewhere looking around for 'em."

"Oh, him—" Helm caught himself quickly. "No matter. We'll find him." He turned back to Gentry, who was looking about in vain for a glimpse of the girl. "Shall we shove off, then?"

Jack gave a slight shrug, but he showed no sign of hanging back. Once started up the canyon, he soon took the lead and kept it. It was he who first spotted Colerain jogging out of an intersecting gulch. It was obvious from Kip's gloomy air that he had been searching fruitlessly for the missing cattle since early in the morning.

The puncher advanced warily, eyeing the pair coldly. "What would you be doing in here?" he demanded.

"More than you—from the looks of things," Gentry retorted genially. "We're on our way now to pick up that Circle C Bar stock—"

"Don't be funny, you!" Colerain was incensed. "If you knew where it was you'd be with it now—traveling away from here fast."

"Not at all. You're the second to make that mistake today." Coldly and with exaggerated politeness Gentry explained what had been happening. "We found the stock with Stevens and offered to drive it home. You can help if you want."

His lofty tone was galling to Kip. Jack was half-a-dozen years older than his own twenty-odd; and Spink was middle-aged. Their superior air of authority made the young fellow acutely conscious of his somehow ignominious position; and he resented their belittling his responsibility for the herd.

"You needn't do anything of the kind," he burst out. "Tell me where the stuff is! I'll see that it gets back on Spade grass— "

Spink laughed lazily. "Run along, boy. Or you can tag along if you insist. We're busy."

Kip jogged angrily in their wake, inwardly fuming. He

was still keenly suspicious that this was a hoax, yet he determined to get to the bottom of it. The two men paid him no further heed as they led the way well up under the massive shadow of the Culebras to the grassy cache deep in the snarl of canyons. Colerain stared with open mouth at the grazing Circle C Bar steers. Not even he could question that they were all here.

The pair gave him no time for questions, starting instead to haze the stock out into the rocky trail and heading it homeward. Colerain found it expedient to combine his efforts with theirs, and in a remarkably short time the recovered beef was clattering down the canyon toward home.

It had been a busy day for the recently hired Lazy Mare hands. It was crowding dusk when they emerged into the lower reaches of Coldwater Canyon with their charges. They turned the steers out with the main herd and went into the house where Madge Pickett was waiting. It took her only a second to spot the triumphant faces of the older men and Kip's crestfallen air.

"Got 'em, did you?" Her tone was indulgent. "Look after those broncs, then, while I get supper on the table."

They agreed readily. Colerain wanted to protest their being welcomed without apparent reservation, but managed to choke it down. The prompt recovery of the stolen stock had not only got him off the hook personally but in all probability had saved his job as well.

The kitchen table was laden with appetizing food, and India was ready to serve them when the men tramped in. Helm Spink sniffed keenly and made for the head of the table. Jack took time to enjoy this sight of the girl, pretty in fresh gingham. She gave Gentry one swift glance and thereafter avoided his eye. Kip noticed this and liked it no better than anything else about the situation.

"Eat hearty, boys." Madge Pickett urged food on them long after their forks began to slow up.

"You're a wonderful cook, ma'am." Spink smacked his lips and rolled his eyes realistically. "Don't know as I ever did taste better cookin'. I can stand a lot of this—till I bust, anyhow."

"Go 'long with you." But Madge was pleased. She pretended not to notice Gentry's persistent efforts to get India to talk. The girl nodded or shook her head, offering the man a spare word or two; after a time she cracked a smile at some pleasantry. But a second later she turned her attention to the glum puncher.

"Have some more pie, Kip," she urged. "You've hardly eaten a thing!"

Her solicitude seemed only to irritate Colerain. He waved the pie away and sank once more into somber abstraction. He was waiting for the other two men to clear out of the house, and it seemed an endless time before the meal was done. Even then Spink deliberately lingered, joshing Mrs. Pickett with what seemed crude familiarity. And India, giving Kip up at last, consented to a grave exchange of opinion with Gentry.

The pair left at last, allowing Colerain to accompany them to the corrals in the cool starlight. They pretended to debate seriously Mrs. Pickett's security here at Spade.

"Hang it all—drop it and go on home," Kip burst out at last, unable to curb his deep exasperation. "Those women've got me, and they don't need you! Don't get too big for your pants just because you were able to do us a favor!"

They laughed at him. "Okay, big boy." Spink was condescending. "We'll let you wrastle this deal. If you need any more help let us know."

The puncher watched their departure in angry silence, but he could not avoid the feeling that somehow he had met with defeat in this day's encounter with the doughty pair.

They were back again the following afternoon, riding in as if completely at home. Kip saw them coming, and he pushed down to meet them, his face stony. "Forget something?" was his markedly unenthusiastic greeting.

They appeared to have decided that the proper way of handling him was not to take him seriously. "Oh, no. We come over to make sure somebody didn't steal you," Gentry told him soberly.

Instantly seething, Colerain tried to block their progress in some way. They coolly refused to be held in conversa-

MAN FROM ROBBER'S ROOST   41

tion, however, and went on toward the house. Kip hung back, and he saw Madge Pickett greet the pair in friendly fashion. They stood about the yard talking for almost an hour. It was small consolation to Colerain that India failed to put in an appearance.

Spink and Gentry left finally, riding off with a jaunty air. Two days later they were back once more, staying even longer this time. Kip, who had been chafing sorely at their cheerful boldness, began to wonder how he could arrange to rid Spade permanently of their unwelcome attentions.

On their third visit the two rode in with India, whom they had met by accident somewhere out on the range. This time the girl chatted freely with them. Kip's bitter mood was not improved by the fact that they actually helped do a certain amount of work on the place.

His torment finally drove him to direct action. Leaving Spade one morning while the nervy pair were making themselves thoroughly at home as usual, Kip struck straight for the Lazy Mare roundup. As luck would have it, Stevens was on the ground.

"Howdy, Colerain," Pat took swift note of the puncher's uneasy sobriety. "How's everything over at Coldwater?"

"Not so good." Kip shook his head. "I suppose you know that Gentry and Spink are over there just about every day pestering the women. In fact, they're over there right now." It had occurred to him that Pat would have something to say about this flagrant waste of time.

"No, I didn't. Glad you mentioned it, though." Pat treated the matter casually and turned the talk to other matters. Kip soon withdrew, satisfied that he had planted the seed which would grow into further action.

He had. That afternoon Stevens rode over to the Spade alone. Colerain's true object was by no means lost on him, and he was curious to see what was going on. Madge Pickett greeted him pleasantly, in noticeable contrast to his last visit, and at his discreet inquiries had only warm praise for the aid and support offered her by Helm Spink and his agreeable friend. Moreover, she did not seem at all bothered by the frequency of their visits. After meeting

India again and drawing the girl out, this time in friendlier circumstances, Pat concluded that jealousy was at work in Colerain's case.

He left at last, his mind easy. He had no intention of speaking to his two hands since situations like this had a way of working themselves out.

Kip, on the other hand, was far from content. It took him two painful days of watching to arrange a private meeting with India. He finally managed to run into the girl by seeming accident in a secluded corner of the canyon where there was no possibility of interruption. By that time he was plainly primed for a showdown. "I've been trying hard to get rid of those Lazy Mare hombres. I know they're a nuisance to you and your mother. But they're awful stubborn."

"A nuisance, Kip?" The girl showed surprise at his determined tone. "How in the world did you gather that? You won't deny they've been a great help to—Mother."

"Well, I know that Gentry's been botherin' you plenty, all the time catching you in corners. He ain't coming here for any other reason, that's sure!"

"He's been very friendly." She was cool. "I don't know what makes you so sure it has annoyed me. Have I said anything to give that impression?"

Kip's face went brick red. Clearly he was deeply wounded. "Oh. Then if I'm butting into something that don't concern me maybe I better quit and pull out—"

"Not at all," she said quickly, stealing a look at his set face. "Certainly nothing I have said could have suggested that. You are . . . quite valuable to us, Kip."

He was exasperated at his utter failure to sound out India's true sentiments. She seemed to blow hot and cold at the same time. "Hanged if I know whether I am or not!" he burst out. "Maybe I'd do well to pay strict attention to my own business!"

"There's no denying there's plenty of work to be done until we can afford more hands to help you," murmured India demurely.

Kip yanked his pony around and raced away in a blind heat. He was wholly at a loss to fathom the girl. She didn't want him to leave, though she could scarcely misinterpret his feelings toward her now. Was she keeping him dangling or was it simply prudence that clung to a good hand in time of need? Colerain couldn't even be assured he was a valuable hand, and his indecision made him miserable.

Meanwhile he pushed himself harder than ever, guarding the stock, keeping it together, and learning the range thoroughly in a short time. Madge finally complained of the endless hours he spent in the saddle and urged him to slack off. Kip wouldn't listen. He was sternly diligent, determined to impress India in spite of herself.

One day less than a week later he was out on the open range where seasoning grass had drawn the Circle C Bar steers. With twilight closing in, Colerain made sure they were in good order and beginning to bed down. He was on the point of turning toward the ranch and supper when a bee buzzed close by his nose. An instant later his startled ears picked up the distant spang of a carbine. Kip stiffened.

"Bees, hell! That was a slug with my name on it!"

A second crack sounded from a different direction, warning of certain odds against him. He did not pack a heavy rifle, and he looked about desperately for cover. Dusk wasn't helping his attackers, nor did it aid him. Moreover, there was little time left if he was to get out of this alive.

Kip would have lost himself on the open swells had not gunfire prevented him from turning that way. He wheeled toward the rising slopes and rammed his spurs in. The treacherous marksmen saluted his flight with a hail of whistling lead. He heard them calling faintly to one another.

Hope surged back as the dark hills loomed up. Peering sharply, Kip made out a shadowy crevice angling upward through the near slope, by means of which it might be possible to slip away. Racing forward at the risk of a nasty fall, he reached its mouth. None too soon! Already he could hear his grim pursuers pounding forward. Their guns crashed and the bullets screamed off the nearby rocks.

Colerain crowded in at the narrow mouth and pressed on. Two minutes later his heart came up into his mouth. Instead of a sure escape route this was a blind gully, and he was trapped.

The renegade attackers seemed to know it quite as soon

as he did. "Come out of that, hombre!" came the mocking call, punctuated by a bouncing slug. "We know you're cornered, and we ain't wasting no time on you!"

Colerain went cold. He was sure he knew that taunting voice. Probably Gentry and Spink had planned things in just this way. The question was, what did they mean to do with him? It would not take long to learn. Turning back with his hands raised, Kip stared astonished in the swiftly fading light at the two utter strangers who crowded close to snatch his gun and take him roughly in charge.

6.

THE LAZY MARE STOCK GATHER had been progressing in fine style. Early in the morning of that same day Zeke Johnson had set a crew to work cutting out three- and four-year-olds for shipment. For greater security Stevens had never confined his stock sales to a single buyer, usually making several deliveries during the course of the season. This particular herd was destined for the shipping pens at Hopewell Junction. Since the cars had been ordered for less than two days hence there could be no slipups and no delays.

Gentry, Spink and the other new hands, who had advanced in Johnson's confidence as a result of their adventure, were assigned the task of driving in the remnants of the most recent gathers from the closed draws and arroyos where the steers were held overnight. It took them to the far corners of the Lazy Mare range; and since they could do their work best in pairs, Jack and his giant companion automatically joined forces.

The two of them were preparing to turn out a dozen wild and sinewy *orejanos* penned in a brush-blocked sandy draw, when Gentry, on the exposed barranca above the impromptu corral, made a sudden futile grab at his hat as it sailed off his head. Swearing hotly, the puncher promptly pivoted his surprised pony and slid down the crumbling dirt bank to join Spink precipitately at the bottom.

"Hunh! If you can't manage that salty bronc—" began Spink disparagingly. Then, getting a glimpse of Jack's grim face, he broke off. "What happened, man?"

"Well, it wasn't the wind that wiped my lid off,"

barked Gentry tersely. He swung to the ground, batting his hat back into shape and tugging it low over his narrowed eyes. Spink saw the jagged rip in its crown. "Whoever turned that slug loose was out for blood!"

"That way, is it?" Spink snorted. "Then what are we waitin' for?"

Drawing rifles from the saddle boot, they set the horses scrambling out of the draw. They avoided exposure while having a circumspect look around, but detected no sign of life or movement. Spink cured this by shoving boldly into the open. A gun promptly cracked from a distant piñon ridge, the bullet stinging his mount to frenzied dancing. Swiftly mastering the animal, the big man rammed it straight in the direction from which the shot had come. Gentry sided him for a hundred yards, then swung off to converge on the ridge from another quarter.

Slugs whined about them but somehow failed to score. Then the gunfire abruptly ceased. Spink grimly took note of the fact without its influencing his determination in the slightest. "We flushed that bird in a hurry," he muttered. "He better hunt his hole or take to flyin'!"

First to top out on the low ridge, he was rewarded by a distant glimpse of the fleeing marksman. Spink whipped his gun up to his cheek and sent several shots whistling after the other just as Gentry pounded forward to rejoin him.

"Who is that?"

"Ain't sure. Looked like Durango from here. If it is, that buckskin of his'll give us a run—"

They delayed no longer, charging down off the far side of the ridge to take up the chase. Though they pushed their horses unmercifully, their attacker raced on far in the lead. The minutes passed, and it was difficult to determine whether they had closed the gap by so much as a yard.

"It could be Durango at that," panted Gentry finally. "If it is, he's just playing with us!" The man and his magnificent horse were both well known to them.

The way led up the rugged slopes of the Culebras. Tipping over the first barrier, the trail plunged into the pine-choked maze beyond. From time to time now they lost sight of the quarry, though he usually tormented them by appearing again, bobbing along at a secure distance.

Helm Spink reined down at last with a curse. "What are we doin'?" he declared forcefully. "This is just playin' that buzzard's game! . . . We're turnin' back."

Gentry looked vaguely startled. "How do you make that out?"

Spink's face was resolute. "You named it, Jack. That smart bird could be playing with us. Hang to his trail and he'll toll us on for miles!" His look was shrewd. "I don't savvy why—but you heard Stevens. That drive to Hopewell starts tomorrow. I aim to be there!"

Jack got it quickly enough and nodded. "If Durango's really anxious for us to come along, he'll wait," he concluded briefly, turning his bronc. "Let's stick to our knitting."

Abruptly abandoning the pursuit, they moved back down the long tangents of the hills. They were a good two hours late when they turned the dozen strays from the draw into the main herd. Fred Sparks was inclined to jeer at their alleged incompetence, without eliciting anything but a wry grin from Spink. Nobody else offered any remarks, and the incident was presently forgotten.

The cutting-out proceeded briskly. By midday Pat knew the trail herd would be ready for the drive with time to spare. Spink and the others did their share of the dusty, grimy labor. Midafternoon saw the cut completed, and the work of slapping on a road brand went forward with dispatch.

By dusk the job was finished, and there remained only the minor chore of night herding before the early morning start of the drive. Gentry and Spink breathed no word of their experience even between themselves; but anyone aware of underlying motives might have noted that they stayed firmly in the midst of the crew. A prowler would have found it impossible to pick them out around the night fire.

Immediately after supper the weary men rolled in. At this advanced season the days were noticeably shorter, and tonight the hours would be curtailed by early rising. Nobody wasted time when Johnson rolled out at four in the morning, bellowing for them to look alive. Belcher had breakfast ready in the chilly darkness. Plates and utensils clattered into the big pan, and mounts were snaked out of the remuda by the time the first rays of dawn appeared in the east.

"Let's have at it, boys! Only way to get a big day behind us is to barge into it." Pat Stevens led the way as they jogged toward the waiting herd, his gauntlets donned and his jacket collar turned up against the nipping frost.

The steers rose from the bed ground, were watered and thrown out on the trail. Rather than cling to the roundabout road, Pat had elected to strike straight east across the open range in the direction of the shipping point. For a mile or two the stock attempted repeatedly to break back, clinging tenaciously to familiar range. It kept the punchers on the hop. Gentry and his friends reveled in this boisterous activity, earning grins and derisive applause by their strenuous exploits in curbing the wayward steers.

"Them boys are born punchers," Ed Lang remarked humorously to Stevens as he paused alongside the other. "Or else they been on a right long vacation the way they pitch into things."

Pat smiled without offering any comment.

The sun rolled over the horizon, easing pinched cheeks and stiffened fingers, and burning the frost rime off the rocks and brush. It promised to be a gorgeous day, mellowed by fall haze. There was just enough breeze blowing up from the south to whip away the dust boiling up from under a thousand hoofs. By midmorning the herd had shaken down into steady plodding travel. From here out it was largely a matter of covering ground.

Though they were scattered about the herd the men found time to meet and exchange a few words from time to time. Tobacco passed from hand to hand, and there was a brisk commerce of humor. In this easy manner Spink and Gentry drifted together.

"Ain't seen a thing of Durango today," Helm muttered, glancing about to make sure their talk could not be overheard.

"No. I've kept an eye peeled too." Jack's gaze roved over the sleeping range, empty except for the moving herd. "He'd be too smart to show himself around this bunch—"

Spink shook his head, frowning. "I ain't so sure. Could

be we had that hombre figured wrong—if it was him," he added in a discontented tone.

Gentry got his meaning completely. "We'll hope so," he grumbled without conviction. "I could be foolish, but I wouldn't like dumping anything like that in Stevens's lap."

"That's right. He's playin' square with us." Spink allowed his pony to drop back while he thoughtfully rolled a smoke. No more was said on the subject then.

Except for allowing the steers a brief rest, midday was ignored. It was Pat's intention to push straight through to Hopewell Junction. During the afternoon it was necessary to negotiate a narrow gap in a low, barren range of hills that barred their progress. The operation took time but was successfully accomplished, and by late afternoon they were drawing ever nearer the shipping point on the railroad.

It would have taken an hour to circle town in order to reach the pens. To drive straight through town could keep them uncommonly busy and was often conducive of excitement; but the help of cheerful visiting cowboys could usually be depended on, and the saving in time would be worthwhile.

"Pull your hats down," Pat cried to the men. "We're going right on through!"

For a time all went well. But as the buildings began to close in the steers grew nervous. They seemed determined to break for the open through any cross alley or vacant lot. Almost at once the punchers found themselves dashing madly this way and that, turning the skittish animals and urging them onward. Ranch rigs hurried out of the street ahead of the rush. Men and women ran back and forth, and kids yelled and ducked. Suddenly the quiet street was filled with uproar from the slap of coiled ropes, the yells of the men, and the dismal bellowing of harried cattle.

For a time it looked as if they might not make it. A rickety ranch rig capsized, and this had to be righted and its enraged owner placated. Steers boiled into a livery yard and had to be chivied out by main strength and meanness. Somehow the center of town was finally negotiated, and they reached the railroad yards where men already had the pen gates open. It was a sweaty, noisy operation before the last of the Lazy Mare stock was hazed into the stout corrals and the gates slammed shut.

A yard engine chugged back and forth, shunting the stock cars into line. Without awaiting instruction the men began punching the steers up the loading chute into the first car. "We made it," Pat remarked to Johnson with quiet satisfaction. "Just nicely in time, too. It'll be dark long before we finish loading."

Johnson nodded. The yellow haze of sunset was already painting the horizon, but he gave it only a glance. It would not be the first time he had finished loading stock cars by the light of coal-oil flares.

The breeze had turned cold with advancing night. Every man who had made the day-long drive was chilly, tired and ravenously hungry. Yet there were no shirkers. Pat saw with approval that Gentry and the other new hands were squarely in the center of things; moreover, they knew exactly what they were doing. Nor were his regular hands to be left behind.

The loading went forward rapidly. Seven o'clock passed unnoticed, and eight came. The yard crew was practiced in this sort of thing. Car after car was briskly loaded and moved out, and the stock in the pens steadily dwindled.

Sam Sloan put in an appearance when the end of the work was well in sight. Eph Sample was not one to overlook the fact. "Where'd you spring from?" he asked the stocky man rudely. "Been hangin' around waitin' till there wasn't no more to do, or what?"

"Shucks, no." Sam refused to take offense. "Cross my heart, Eph, I meant to come along with the drive—and then went and plumb forgot it! Wait till yuh get my age," he grinned at Sample, who topped him by a good ten years. "You'll learn how easy it is for hard work t' slip your mind!"

Sample turned away huffily. "Fresh young sprout," he growled, oblivious of the grins of listening men.

Sam plunged headlong into the loading, grabbing a prod pole and hustling the stock up the chute with the others. Fresh as he was, he put on a show of energy which drew catcalls of derision from the weary Lazy Mare hands.

When the count for that car was complete, Pat slammed the sliding door shut on the bawling beeves and signaled to the waiting brakie to spot the final car. The loaded cars

MAN FROM ROBBER'S ROOST 51

were waiting in a coupled string with an engine at its head. Pat began to glance around for some sign of the consignee's representative. The man had agreed to be here today in time to close the deal and take charge of the shipment, and thus far he had failed to put in an appearance. Some reps were casually inclined to cut it fine, however, preferring to remain out of the smell and cinder dust, so that Pat was not particularly concerned.

The last car banged and screeched into place, and the men hurried the last score or so of steers into the chute. There was work here for only three or four men, and Johnson had the windup well in hand. Stevens motioned Spink over to where he was standing.

"Call your boys off," he instructed, smiling. "You did fine, and this is your chance to grab a break. Turn up at the Lazy Mare tomorrow night, Spink, and I don't care what you do in the meantime."

Hagen and Sparks greeted the welcome news with pleasure. "Let's go, Gentry!" They hailed Jack peremptorily, already getting their broncs up. As he passed the same word on to his regular crew, Pat did not miss how speedily the four grasped this opportunity to make themselves scarce.

The last three or four head were being crowded aboard with shouts of gratification from the few remaining hands, when Stevens noted the sudden reappearance of Spink and Jack. They jogged down the beaten lane reluctantly, their full attention on him. Helm got down and came forward, his manner diffident. Pat saw in a flash what was wrong. There probably wasn't enough money between them at the moment to finance the anticipated bust.

Pat faced Spink squarely, giving no sign that he guessed their dilemma. "Well. Do you boys hate to part with work, or what?" he quizzed.

Spink stood first on one foot and then the other, avoiding Pat's twinkling eye. "Now—uh, boss," he began in an embarrassed tone. "The fact is—"

Pat let him come to a full stop, then chuckled. "I get it," he said indulgently. "You unexpectedly find yourselves a little short at the moment. Is that it?"

Spink's face cleared. "You've hit it, Stevens. We don't

aim to be grabby; but if you could see your way to advance us a few dollars, it'll be fine."

Pat put his hand in his pocket, glancing toward the last car. It was loaded, and Johnson himself was fastening the hasp on the closed door. He was just in the act of stepping back when the couplings of the loaded string abruptly took up the slack with a grinding jerk. Slowly the train began to move.

"Hold on!" Pat yelled, forgetting Spink and everything else as he sprang forward. "Where are they going with those cars? There's no release on this stock yet! The deal hasn't been closed!"

Despite his indignant outcry and the little Johnson and the remaining men could do, the train continued to roll ponderously on. In a minute or two it would clear the loading pens.

"Get hold of those trainmen!" Pat shouted. "Tell them to signal that engineer or throw on the air! I want that stock held right here till I give the word!"

But no one acknowledged his orders, and the train trundled on with slowly gathering momentum. At the last minute they saw a figure racing toward them along the ballast. It was the fireman, they discovered as he burst hatless into the flickering light of the smoky flares.

"My God, Stevens! There's hell to pay," the man gasped, his face pasty. "Three strangers climbed on the engine! They slugged Murph—I jumped before they could put a slug in me! They know how to run that teakettle, and they're stealing the train!"

Pat listened open-mouthed. It did not take him long to gather what was happening. This had never been heard of before, to his knowledge; yet it was a bold new style of rustling, and no mistake! At that very moment a string of warning shots crackled derisively from the engine as it drew rapidly off into the night—spelling an eloquent goodbye to his herd.

7.

THE BLAZING WORDS were hardly out of the fireman's mouth before Helm Spink began to move. He pivoted around and swung smoothly into his saddle, kicking the surprised bronc into swift motion. Gentry swept up beside him, and together they raced after the rapidly accelerating stock train. It was done so easily that the pair seemed automatically to work in unison.

Whoever had commandeered the engine knew how to get the best out of it. Only a surprise move could have enabled them to start the heavy string of cars rolling fast enough for a clean getaway. The renegades had not foolishly risked an appearance at the rear end. This fact alone facilitated the success of Spink's and Gentry's plan.

They were forced to race their horses cruelly to catch up at all, but steadily the distance narrowed between them and the last car. It was Gentry who risked disaster by boldly jumping his mount across the rails. An instant later he drew up beside the swaying steel ladder at the rear end of the car as Spink closed in on the other side.

They sped close alongside for a while. Then Gentry swung agilely out of the saddle, his feet slapping firmly on the bottom rung. Almost at once Spink followed suit. They were grimly climbing the unsteady ladders toward the roof of the car, no more than vague blots in the gloom, when the tail of the lurching train swung around a rocky spine and disappeared from view.

Pat had never witnessed greater presence of mind or swifter action. Taking a cue from the pair, he ran swiftly toward the station to report this incredible event to the agent. It might still be possible to halt the train at some remote switch. It was by no means certain, despite the new hands' success in catching the runaway string on the fly, that this dangerous attempt to recapture the herd would prove successful.

He might have changed his mind had he been with the pair. Some impulse stronger than mere adventurous daring drove them as they hauled themselves out on top of the rumbling rear car and started methodically to work their way forward.

"Durango's mine if he turns up, Gentry, and don't yuh forget it!" Spink shouted in Jack's ear. "This is pretty much our own doing! We don't owe them wolves a thing from here on out!"

Gentry nodded briefly, not pausing in his precarious advance. The cars were rolling now at considerable speed, swaying and jerking, forcing the two men to crouch on their hands and knees as they clutched the catwalk. Negotiating the last car, they managed to swing across to the next. Their progress was slow but steady. Jack paused once to stare ahead over the shadowy tops.

"Reckon they know we're aboard?" he asked tightly.

Spink wasn't sure. "They'll have a look wherever they stop. They must be making for some desert loadin' chute." He thought briefly. "It'll pay out to hit before they get that far along—"

A long straight space of track enabled them to rise and run down the length of several cars before an unexpected lurch almost threw Spink hurtling into the gulf of darkness. Gentry yanked him down, clutching a rattling brake wheel for support. They forged steadily onward.

Their failure to meet any one of the stock thieves working his way back over the tops encouraged their hopes of a grim surprise. Long as it seemed, it was only a matter of tense minutes before Jack silently pointed out the coal tender immediately ahead.

Now came the critical juncture. It was only too possible that the watching renegades might see them coming in the red glare from the firebox door. Fortunately the engine had been recently coaled up, and the fuel rose in a high mound, cutting off the direct view from the cab.

MAN FROM ROBBER'S ROOST 55

The pair boldly risked serious injury by leaping down into the darkness of the heaped tender. They made it safely. Crouching there in the coal, they drew their guns and listened to the hoarse voices of apparently jubilant men. A careful look ahead showed them three shadowy figures going about the work of running the engine, peering backward every now and then from gangway or cab window but obviously otherwise unconcerned.

Spink thrust his head close to Gentry's. "Take your side of the pile—and don't miss a trick! A slug or two'll show 'em we mean business!"

They scrambled instantly to positions, the clank of metal and hiss of steam covering both their words and furtive movements. The first warning the renegades received was the roar of the gunshot directly behind the shadowy cab. A slug struck the vibrating Johnson bar and screamed out the cab window.

"Hoist 'em, you!"

Spink's guttural command electrified the bandits and froze them in their tracks. Gentry blasted a shot at the steel-plated floor from his side of the tender for emphasis, the bullet buzzing about the iron enclosure like an outraged bee.

This was more than enough. The surprised trio slowly elevated their hands as an abandoned coal scoop clattered hollowly. Three set faces turned cautiously, the eyes glazed and blank.

"Is that you, Spink?" The burly man who had replaced the engineer spoke up in a mildly accusing tone.

"Shut up! And stop this thing," Helm spat. "Jump, now! . . . One word out o' you, Blacky," he warned savagely when the other tried to speak, "and you'll finish talking through the top of your head!"

"Hang it all, Spink! Yuh ought t' be with us—" protested another man.

Helm silenced him with a blow across the mouth. He was secretly furious at not finding with them the man called Durango. "No talk!" he threatened as Gentry quickly relieved them of their weapons. "I want this tin can heading backwards in nothing flat. *You hear me?*"

Blacky scowlingly braked the engine to a halt. Clearly

he understood its operation, for a moment later steam screeched and the ponderous drive wheels began to reverse. The train moved slowly at first and the couplings of the heavy stock cars protested shrilly, then it gradually increased speed.

Little was said as the train industriously puffed back over the mile or two it had covered. Jack saw to it that the boiler was fired, then backed his two charges into a corner of the cab. Presently the dull glow of Hopewell Junction's main street showed in the night sky over the silhouetted backs of the cars. The train chugged deliberately into the yards, to be met by a clamoring crowd of men as the engine ground to a halt.

Pat Stevens was the first to swing aboard the cab. Sheriff Rawlins followed, disputing precedence with Sam Sloan immediately behind him. "Good work, Spink!" The Lazy Mare owner was grimly approving as he noted the glowering prisoners. "You and Gentry did a fine job here. It won't be overlooked."

His words were not without design, for the chunky Hopewell Junction lawman gave the two a single brief glance and then turned his attention to their captives.

"What kind of a game is this?" demanded Rawlins harshly. "Tamperin' with railroad property—not to mention a whole trainload of beef! You hombres wouldn't be hungry, would yuh?" he added sarcastically.

"All right. You can take charge of them now, Rawlins," Pat broke in. "From the sound of that crowd, you may need help—"

Word of the bold theft had spread rapidly through town. Just about every able-bodied man available had put in an appearance, and most of them seemed to feel personally called upon to do violence to the culprits. There were angry voices raised; and the glare of lanterns and track flares revealed a mass of gesticulating men around the engine.

Suddenly a handful of railroad men pushed briskly through the mob. A heavy set official swung up on the cab step. It was Superintendent McNally of the Pueblo Division.

"Put those men in jail, Fred," he ordered tersely in a rumbling tone, his steady glance fixed on Rawlins. "The road has first claim in the theft of property entrusted to its care, and I intend to prefer charges at once."

"There must have been some funny work here," another railroad man exclaimed above the general clamor. "Murphy, the engineer, was picked up unconscious. He's badly hurt. What became of his fireman? We'll want him on the carpet!"

"Where is Taggart? He was here!" Townsmen and busybodies immediately began a search for the luckless fireman, only adding to the confusion.

Rawlins was already beginning dimly to sense looming difficulties in the handling of his prisoners. "What do you think I'm doin, Jake?" He was irritable. "Get some of your railroad gang here in a hurry. Dammit, man, I'll have to run the gauntlet through that mob—"

"Ease off, Sheriff. My crew is handy," advised Pat. "We'll see that these birds get over to the jail so fast no one'll know what's happening."

Despite his prediction the angry crowd hampered their movements materially as they hustled the prisoners down off the engine to the ground. The Lazy Mare hands and all the available trainmen were only partially successful in forming a cordon.

A shout greeted the appearance of Spink and Jack Gentry as they climbed down from the engine in the flickering red glare. "There they are! By gravy, that's our boys!" a man cried enthusiastically. There was an ominous rumble in the cheer that followed, but it seemed directed at the captives.

Sam had managed to squeeze himself close to Pat's side. He listened to the cries of admiration and approval for the nervy pair with a cynical droop of his underlip. "If this deal was arranged for show," he managed to make himself heard by the younger man, "it was pretty shrewd management!"

Pat was unaffected by this suspicion. "Don't be too sure of that, Sam." He had long since become fully aware of a sinister undercurrent in the activities of his new hands. But there could be little doubt that the feat they had just witnessed was real.

This certainly was justified only a moment later. As

Sheriff Rawlins endeavored to thrust his prisoners toward the jail through the mob, the man called Blacky took sudden advantage of the hampering crowd. He ducked, jerked free of his guard and began to worm vigorously away through the packed mass.

Helm Spink, who had not been more than a few feet away from the renegade since the latter's capture, did not hesitate in this tangle. He whipped out his Colt and fired point-blank an instant before Blacky would have succeeded in disappearing.

Men yelled and struggled, waving their fists. But the slug found its mark. In the midst of the uproar, Blacky went down with a hoarse cry. He was pulled up barely able to navigate, with blood streaming down his leg.

"Try that again, blast you, and it'll be your head!" Spink roared. His savage anger made the crowd fall back. Not even Superintendent McNally protested as Spink and Fred Sparks hauled the wounded man roughly along. Getting the shrinking prisoners to the jail and securely locked up was a touch-and-go affair. Fortunately most of the enthusiasm of the crowd was directed solely toward the intrepid pair who had effected the capture.

Helm and Jack were slapped on the back repeatedly with jovial friendliness. But they frowned as they shrugged off these well-intentioned advances, nor did they respond to the many who came up to them eagerly. The pair always liked to avoid attention in town, a circumstance amply demonstrated in Dutch Springs, and Pat realized how awkward they found this situation.

After the captives were safely locked up, and McNally and the other railroad officials had paid their brusque compliments, Pat made a point of cornering Spink for a word in private.

"You made short work of that ambitious steal," he told the self-conscious puncher frankly. "Whoever Blacky's crowd is, they never figured on you and Gentry!"

Helm listened, brooding. "Ain't so sure of that. We weren't even supposed to be here tonight, Stevens!" he blurted. "Unless I'm way off my rocker, this business was planned with considerable care. Somebody tried to make sure we'd never be on the spot at all!"

MAN FROM ROBBER'S ROOST

Pat detected far more significance in the words than the other could have intended, but he gave no sign of his discovery. "I'm not dead sure that I follow you," was all he said, masking his deep interest.

Spink hesitated awkwardly. "Yuh may recall how long it took Jack and me to bring in that bunch of long-haired stuff yesterday mornin'," he said finally. "There was a reason for it. We was fired on by some skunk with a carbine rifle. We took after him, o' course—but he was ready for that. Took us quite a few miles to wake up to the fact that we'd never nab him on that fast horse he was straddlin'. It sure turned out a streak o' lightnin', and no mistake!"

Pat weighed this curious story soberly. "And you figure it was a play to tell you and Gentry off—maybe even make you miss the drive. Is that it?"

Helm shrugged. "Soon as we seen that bronc was shod we turned back. It was probably a blooded horse—just some more of that careful plannin' I mentioned." He looked away. "I could be wrong, Stevens, but I won't conceal from yuh that's how I see it."

Pat had made up his mind how to approach the whole delicate topic, and he spoke out now without pulling any punches. "Spink, I can't help but think you feel that you and Gentry pulled this affair down on me—accidentally, I'll admit." He eyed the other squarely. "Just how well do you really know Blacky and his pals?"

Helm hastily averted his glance. "Well, I've heard of 'em," he confessed with marked constraint. "But you're dead wrong about there being any reason for 'em hitting at us, Stevens. I ain't quite got it figured out myself." His defense was stout, and he appeared sensitive on the subject.

But Pat was not satisfied. "If that's the case, don't it seem queer they picked you and Jack out of all my crew to toll away just at this time?"

Spink scowled. "Maybe it is. Anyhow, if yuh make more sense out of it than I can you're doing good!"

Pat shook his head. "I still think this business hooks up with that shooting in Dutch Springs the day I hired you fellows. There were those Circle C Bar steers you got accused of rustling, too. I don't get the exact connection,

I'll grant. But it's a mistake to assume such things as that can be purely accidental.''

Spink stubbornly remained silent. Pat, however, refused to let it go at that. "If you were to name anyone, who would you guess was behind all these doings?" he persisted, trying to pin the man down.

But Spink had clammed up for good. "Don't know," he denied briefly, looking up hopefully as Sam Sloan came waddling forward to join them.

"Here's the hero now," the little man jibed lightly, squinting up at Helm in the familiar manner of a fighting bantam. "How come yuh ain't getting in on all the free drinks? Cheapest load you'll ever take aboard!"

Helm scarcely heard him. "How about it, Stevens? Is it okay if me and Gentry take off for the ranch? I'm plumb sick of all this crazy speculatin'," he added gruffly.

Pat covered the moment smoothly, waving a casual assent. "Suit yourselves. I'll see you there."

He and Sloan watched the giant stride off. Sam's eye glinted shrewdly. "I don't know what yuh got yourself tangled up in, boy—but those birds are owlhoots, sure as you're born!"

Pat met his gaze with a light smile. 'Think so, do you?"

"Dang right! Oh, I know what you're goin' to say. They don't act like it—now. But you'll wake up with a bang, Stevens! . . . Man, the laugh me and Ez'll have on you when that happens!"

Pat let him have it now by offering no retort.

8.

IT WAS OBVIOUS that Spink and his pals were frankly uneasy within sight and hearing of the law. Even Gentry appeared anxious to get away before Sheriff Rawlins had a better chance at him. Sparks and Hagen had already quietly disappeared. It did not escape Stevens that they must be afraid the train robbers might talk too much.

Pat was forced to look after a hundred irksome details as a result of the night's adventure. Once done with the law, he was able to track down the buyer's agent and complete the sale of the cattle, thus ending his own responsibility for the stock.

Finishing his work at a late hour, he left the Stockmen's Hotel with the welfare of his crew in mind. He did not need to be reminded that almost the entire town was hilariously celebrating the capture of the renegades. In the absence of Gentry and Spink, the Lazy Mare hands were basking in reflected glory.

Almost the first persons he ran into were Sam Sloan and Johnson. The foreman was watchfully patrolling the street with the same idea as Pat's in mind.

"Hanged if these rough-barked punchers ain't worse to ride herd on than a bunch of cows, Stevens," he groused. "But everything's in hand—up to the present." Beyond a fistfight or two he had no serious incidents to report.

Fights were not uncommon, but Pat was interested. It did not astonish him that rumors about Helm Spink and Gentry were current, which the Lazy Mare punchers promptly resented.

"They're sayin' them two got jobs with yuh to arrange

that steal—and then threw down their pals at the last minute," informed Sam maliciously.

Pat brushed this aside. "Better get the boys headed for home as soon as you decently can," he advised Johnson. "There's nothing more for us here."

He and Sam retired at a late hour to the hotel, where they put up for the night. The foreman was not seen again, and by morning all evidence of Lazy Mare stock horses had disappeared from the Hopewell Junction hitch racks. The crew had pulled out. After a final conference with Sheriff Rawlins, Pat turned his back on the Junction. He and Sam made a leisurely trip to Dutch Springs, and it was well into the afternoon when Stevens arrived once more at his ranch.

With the roundup over the crew was all once more at headquarters. A change had occurred overnight in their attitude toward Gentry and Spink. As a result of their loyalty to the brand no longer being seriously questioned, they had been taken heartily into the ranch family; and although the warmth of their welcome was unobtrusive it was couched in a language which they were all equipped to understand.

Practical jokes of the most atrocious character were painstakingly devised to play on them, and they were included in the jests and confidences of the others. Only those who had suffered the abuse and indifference of men for a long time could appreciate what this meant to the pair.

It was a period when work would be slack till the task of riding the winter range loomed close. Spink and Gentry took prompt advantage of the situation by riding over to Coldwater Canyon. Here their welcome was no less genuine. Madge Pickett had heard of their exploit, and this warmhearted woman subjected them to considerable embarrassment by pretending that the law would soon be seeking their services as a result of their recent activities.

Spink in particular squirmed under her officious attentions, yet he seemed to enjoy it too. He and Madge were soon on terms of great familiarity; and though India watched developments with whimsical resignation, she had no real protest to make either to her mother or to Gentry, who certainly gave her full opportunity to speak her mind.

Pat Stevens knew all about the preoccupation of his two hands, without showing the slightest concern for the results. He had talked with Ezra in connection with the Picketts, and knew the extent of the old rawhide's curiosity, to say nothing of Sam Sloan's cool effrontery where other people's affairs were concerned.

He was not disappointed. Ezra came riding in to the Lazy Mare that evening. He immediately sought Pat out and took him aside mysteriously. Pat pretended to have no idea what he was about.

"Now what are you wasting my time over?" he grunted absently.

Ez glared at him with his single eye. "I suppose yuh know where Spink and Gentry are spendin' their time again," he opened up significantly.

"Over at Mrs. Pickett's you mean—"

If Pat counted on taking the wind out of the lanky redhead's sails, he was not successful. "That's right—over at Spade," affirmed Ez tersely. "Wouldn't you say them two ought t' know what's goin' on over there?"

"Offhand, yes . . . Of course cows aren't what either of them have on their minds right now." Pat's eyes twinkled. "What makes you ask that, Ezra?"

"Ain't they told yuh nothin' at all?"

"No."

"Hunh! Can't see why. They must know young Colerain's been missin' for near two days. Ain't no mistake about it, Stevens. I put myself in the way of that girl after I caught on—and she told me the boy ain't been seen. She's some considerable worried!"

Pat could not understand this. "And Jack and Helm Spink haven't done anything? They must know about it."

"They been tellin' them women not to fret—that young Kip's either sulkin' somewheres or has quit and pulled away for good."

Pat pondered the information soberly. "I see their point, at that," he allowed. "They could be right. Colerain *has* been downright jealous of that pair."

"Then how about them?" The big man was sharp. "They jealous enough of *him* to put him away?"

Pat immediately shook his head. "I'll never believe it. I won't accuse them of anything of that kind, Ez. All the same, this is worth looking into. Is it too much to ask you to keep an eye open for a while over there at Coldwater?"

Except on the rare occasions when he got his back up Ezra was in the habit of accepting Pat's lightest request as an order, and this time was no different from the others.

"Colerain may turn up again, in which case we'll do well to keep our fingers out of the deal," Stevens continued. "Meanwhile I'll keep my ear to the ground at this end and see what I can pick up."

They talked a few minutes longer before Ezra pulled away for home. Not ten minutes after he left Spink and Gentry rode in from some jaunt of their own. Pat scarcely needed to ask where they had been; and he was satisfied that the two were unaware of his own conference with Ezra. Wary by instinct, they might immediately have guessed its import.

Pat came up to them the following morning, careful to make no reference to Spade, waiting meanwhile to see if either man would bring up the subject of Colerain's strange disappearance. Nothing of the kind occurred.

He stopped Spink as the latter was on the point of riding away from the ranch. "By the way, Spink. If you should happen to see the Picketts, pass the word along that I'd like young Colerain to drop over here sometime," he said quietly.

Helm gave him a startled glance, then dropped his eyes. His nod was wooden. "I'll do that, Stevens." Obviously he did not intend to divulge any of his private knowledge.

Pat's lips compressed. He let the man go, noting that Gentry joined the other by a roundabout way as they started off across the range. During the morning he did plenty of thinking and was ready for the pair by the time they returned. He called Spink into the ranch house kitchen immediately after the noon meal.

"Sit down." Finishing his coffee, he waved Helm to a seat across the table. "I haven't seen young Kip. Did he show up yet?" he demanded directly.

Spink understood him completely. He did not shock easily, but his response was slow. "No, Stevens, he hasn't." A frown furrowed his thick brows. "I'm beginning to wonder myself what's become of him—"

Pat studied the man narrowly. "Haven't you any idea at all?"

"Why, no." The other looked surprised.

"Sure of that, are you?"

Helm froze, regarding him grimly.

"Just what are you drivin' at?"

Pat waved his hand impatiently. "Here we are, back where we started. If you'll tell me exactly what you think happened to Colerain, Spink, I'm fully satisfied that we'll locate him that much sooner."

Helm's headshake was barely perceptible. "Don't know a thing about him, Stevens; and what's more, I haven't an idea. Sorry."

"Nonsense. Let's be plain about this. Next thing I know you'll be claiming you're not on the dodge—"

"Who, me? Hang it, Stevens, if you want me to take my time and go, I will."

"Didn't say that. Didn't mean it, either." Pat looked at him speculatively. "If you don't want to talk about yourself, then, let's start on your enemies."

"My what?" Helm might never have recognized the word. Certainly his sparring was of a superior order. "Hell, boss! If I got any at all they don't even know where I am!"

"I'll buy that," Pat retorted evenly, "if you'll name a few just to play square."

The rugged giant lurched to his feet, his heavy features contorted in disgust. "You don't want me," he announced decidedly. "I reckon Madge Pickett can use a good man, though. I'll ride over and see."

"No. You'll stay here, Spink." Pat could be equally final. "Closemouthed as you seem to be about it—and about yourself—others have heard of Kip Colerain's turning up missing. As a matter of fact, Sheriff Lawlor wants to talk to you. He may ride out later tonight—or he could even show up this afternoon."

This warning had been devised on the spur of the moment since Pat had no remote hint of what Lawlor's ideas were on the subject or whether he even knew about it. Yet the shot told. Spink sank heavily back into his chair, his expression one of defeat and chagrin.

"Damn the man! What in time can he want with me?" he almost groaned.

"You ought to know. He won't ask you the questions I have. He won't have to. He'll *tell* you—and you'll listen."

Helm spread his thick hands, a trapped look in his eyes. "All right, yuh got me. I have hit the long trail a time or two, Stevens—and swung a wide loop, for that matter."

"You and Gentry, that is." Pat nodded. "You *are* pals, I take it?"

Spink's reluctant assent was guarded. "In a manner of speakin'—"

"Oh, now. You're not giving anything away," Pat encouraged him easily. "I had the four of you figured from the day you signed on. You're all one gang, aren't you?"

Spink's defenses were crumbling rapidly. His fleeting grin was somewhat shamefaced. "You got us pegged, Stevens. We're part of the Robber's Roost bunch, or was—" He halted, fearful of revealing more than he bargained for. "but I swear we didn't figure on bringin' you none of that mess!"

Pat nodded. "And what persuaded you to pull away and come here—if that isn't water over the dam?"

The giant hesitated. "Too many bosses, yuh might say. We got plumb fed up."

"I see. Driven out, eh?"

The thrust was shrewd, as Spink's averted glance attested. "Just how sure are you the rest of that bunch haven't decided to haunt you?" Pat pressed.

"No, no! Nothing like that. For one thing, it ain't worth their while," Spink denied swiftly. "We just decided to play it straight, Stevens—you can make up your mind whether we have here in Powder Valley! . . . We don't ask for nothing more." He was frankly persuasive now. Then he looked baffled. "But it won't work. They pinch you for not walkin' a chalk line; and when you try, they grab you anyway! I know you think it's funny, Stevens—all the things that've been going on. It'd look different if we wasn't around. Maybe we better pull up stakes and drift."

"Not a bit of it." Pat was firm. "This thing may take some ironing out, Spink; but if you go on as you are, you'll be safe here. I'll undertake to stall the law off if you can manage to deal with your—friends."

Spink showed hearty relief at his expression of confidence. "I didn't make no mistake about you, Stevens! You know what we're up against—and we won't forget it," he exclaimed.

Pat allowed him to choose what he would say on the subject to the others, and the rest of that day things went along much as usual. But the next afternoon Ezra rode in at full speed and accosted the Lazy Mare owner.

"Seems crazy to go on reportin' this disappearing act," he began gruffly. "But from where I stand it's happened again!"

"Not the girl?" Pat asked swiftly, fearing the worst.

"Shucks, no," the one-eyed man quickly relieved his anxiety. "But she's dang nigh the only one left!" he broke off. "I expect yuh know Spinks' been busy makin' his play for Madge Pickett all this time?"

"I guessed it, anyway."

"Well, he's made his point," Ezra ventured shrewdly. "He's been ridin' the old girl around the range a lot lately—and now it looks like the pair of 'em have pulled out. Eloped!" Ezra's disgust at this knew no bounds.

"Eloped! How sure are you of that?" demanded Pat incredulously.

Ez shrugged. "Ain't. But they been gone since late yesterday afternoon. That girl's pretty near frantic with Colerain missing and all—and when two old fools disappear that way, what would you make of it yourself?"

Pat was forced to concede the logic of this reasoning. At the same time he found the unexpected development incredible. With the cynicism of greater age, however, Ezra had already abandoned the possibility of any sane explanation.

"No use sayin' Miz Pickett wouldn't never abandon her daughter that way," he pointed out sourly. "She's a single woman and she's pushin' fifty. When her kind falls for a man, she goes for him whole hog," he announced dogmatically. "What I can't figure out is what Spink can be thinkin' of. Yuh don't reckon he aimed to turn India over to that Gentry?"

Pat shook his head. "Now I think about it, I've an idea what might have made him take out, at that." In a lowered tone he explained what he had learned about Spink's past. "In spite of his claims to the contrary, I'm satisfied the Robber's Roost crowd are closing in on him and his friends. Spink may well have decided it was high time to move out. But it was foolish to drag that woman into any such deal."

Ezra thought this over. "If they're owlhoots, Lawlor alone would be enough to give them hombres a case of itchy feet. It was plain from the first they didn't want no part of the law."

"I'm not sure about Gentry—but Sparks and Trap Hagen are still around," pursued Pat thoughtfully. "Would this mean that Spink's given them all the brush-off?"

"Huh! Now it's started," Ezra predicted, "it won't be long before they all do a fade, mark my words, boy."

He would have said more. But at that moment the clatter of hard-driven hoofs turned them sharply, and a grim-faced horseman pounded into the yard. To their astonishment they saw that it was Kip Colerain, minus his hat and breathless with some significant message.

9.

"WHAT DO YOU WANT WITH ME?" had been Colerain's first indignant words when he understood that the two rough strangers meant to make him a prisoner. He had never laid eyes on the pair before, and there could be no reason for their interest in his movements unless they mistook him for someone else.

"Shut up, kid," he was told peremptorily. "The less fuss you make, the better we'll get along—I'm tellin' yuh now!"

The very brevity of the statement carried a deadly threat. Kip's hands were bound tighter than there was any need for, and his legs fastened underneath the horse. Then his captors turned the bronc and set off through the shadowy dusk. Colerain somehow managed to swallow his anger and to follow every move alertly. The complete mystery of these events challenged his furious thoughts. What was behind it all?

The hard-faced renegades, now moving lazily along, turned back into the hills and soon followed a trail that wound through pine and scrub cedar. They appeared coolly sure of their way. It was clear that Kip's sudden capture had been the sum of their duties for the present.

Was it possible these men had some connection with the raiders of the Circle C Bar herd who had been nabbed by Ezra and Sam Sloan? It seemed hardly worth their trouble to get revenge this way—unless they were contemplating a fresh attack on the herd and, determined this time to effect a clean getaway, were intent on putting Kip out of circulation beforehand. This possibility gave rise to further uneasy speculation. Was he the only one on whom their sights were leveled? And what were they going to do with him? It would be little to their advantage if they were to turn him loose afterward with his knowledge of their identity.

Kip's blood ran cold at the thought of what this could mean. They could very well be taking him into the hills now so that his body would never be found to incriminate them. It was more than enough to make him gloomy and tight-lipped, and he had trouble fighting down his alarm.

Darkness fell and the stars came out as the three pushed on into wild and unfrequented country. Colerain was not sufficiently familiar with this range to figure out except in a general way where he was being taken. Time passed, and the evening chill took on an edge. It was late when his captors rode into a grassy hollow far up on the Culebra flanks, where a tumble-down log line cabin loomed up darkly.

"Fire's out," one of the renegades muttered, then raised his voice in a harsh call. "Blacky! Dang it, are yuh asleep in there already—?"

After a moment there was a thumping noise in the cabin, and a burly figure shadowed the doorway. "You, Clabe?" An enormous yawn followed. "Took you long enough . . . Any luck at all?"

The answer was a grunt. Kip's captors had dismounted to unsaddle and turn their ponies loose. "Hooked our fish . . . Kick that fire alive, will yuh? And fix us a bite to eat."

Now that his eyes were accustomed to the gloom, the man called Blacky stepped forward to peer at Colerain, who was still bound securely astride his mount. "Do it yourselves," he retorted. "Is this him—?" He began to curse disgustedly. "Why, it ain't nothin' but a kid! . . . What kind of a gag are you boys pulling here?"

Clabe Turner stirred up the dying fire by tossing a few chunks on, then turned in the flickering light. "He's that Circle C Bar puncher," he announced flatly. "We didn't ask him for no birth certificate. Yuh wanted him here. So what?"

Blacky tugged at the knots of Kip's bonds, hauling him unceremoniously to the ground. Despite twinges of pain, the puncher maintained a bleak silence. The cool way

MAN FROM ROBBER'S ROOST 71

these men addressed one another and their hard faces warned him of just how tough they were.

Releasing Colerain, Blacky surveyed him with contempt. "Humph! You ain't much to look at. I'll admit I ain't much sold on dogs and wet-eared punks." His heavy eyes glared at Kip. "Make yourself small around here, kid—and don't try to do no sneak."

Chafing his raw wrists, Colerain turned slowly to the fire and sank down on a stump. He did not need to be told that he was in dangerous company. The renegades somberly brewed coffee and fried fatback at the fire, ignoring him completely.

Kip glanced about. A ragged gully, weird in the dancing light, bisected this hollow in the hills. The sagging line cabin stood on a bench, which, though narrow at its edge, thickened farther off and was backed by a fringe of pines. The work corrals behind the place had been more or less broken up for firewood over the years, and it was plain the camp had been abandoned for some time. Kip's heart sank. Small likelihood of any drifting line rider discovering his dilemma!

"When'll Durango be back?" the third renegade asked out of a lengthy silence, his mouth full of food.

"Not till he finishes what he's got to do and reports to Palmer," Blacky tossed back indifferently. "What do you care, Carnes?"

Jip Carnes shrugged, finishing off his steaming coffee gustily. "Don't. I figure Palmer had this deal blueprinted before we left the Roost."

"So what are you worryin' about? You done your part—so far." It was obvious from his authoritative tone that Blacky had constituted himself leader of these men.

"Well—Durango's slated to take care of Spink and that chesty Jack, ain't he?" Carnes argued. "I can't see how one man's aiming to deal with that pair and make it stick . . . O' course Lant Palmer must have that figured too—and he don't leave much to chance."

"Forget it then. You ain't got a thing to bother you till we tackle that Lazy Mare herd. Once we close that deal, Spink and Gentry will be sick of the name of Powder Valley!"

Colerain sat there petrified, his scalp crawling at the coolness with which they discussed their brazen plans in front of him. It grew plainer by the minute that they did not expect him to carry away word of what he heard.

"Palmer's a sharp customer, all right," commented Tanner. "He must've gone to some trouble to learn this Stevens's business. Must be some railroad men mixed up in it too, if this thing works the way it's planned."

"Told you I've got that all taken care of, didn't I?" Blacky silenced him sharply. "You birds are all alike. The way you crab about the details of every job it's a wonder you ain't runnin' things!"

They continued to bicker irritably. Colerain knew enough of owlhoots to recognize the result of tightly strung nerves. These men were involved in some bold project.

What could they want of him—except to join him with Gentry and Spink as a scapegoat on whom to lay the blame for their crime. Even in his agitation he understood that the two punchers were probably the victims of organized enmity in much of what had happened lately. His own predicament loomed so large, however, that he had scant sympathy to waste on anyone besides himself.

Blacky stood up at last, stretching and yawning once more. "All right—inside, you." He jerked his head toward the cabin, his eyes fastened on Kip. "We'll get some shut-eye. And we want to find you here come morning. I think we will."

"Don't I eat?" Colerain bristled, trying to pretend that he found nothing alarming in their talk.

"Your arm ain't broke." Gesturing indifferently, the big renegade indicated the scraps left in the greasy pan and the dregs remaining in the cold coffeepot.

Kip salvaged a few mouthfuls, largely for the sake of appearances, and moved toward the old cabin. Finding an unclaimed bunk, he tumbled in. The others retired sullenly, making no attempt to post a guard. Silence settled over the wilderness camp, broken only by the melancholy hoot of an owl and the muted cropping of grass outside by the horses.

The puncher entertained no expectation of sleeping—his brain was whirling hopelessly. Useless to dream of warning Pat Stevens or anyone else of imminent catastrophe! These men did not intend that he should slip away. Even to try to shift his position in this creaking bunk would bring them to their feet with blazing guns.

It was a long time before Kip suddenly dozed off, his brain weary with fruitless searching. He awoke seemingly at once, with pale light seeping in at the sagging door. He lifted his head cautiously to find Clabe Tanner sitting on the edge of his own bunk, looking over at him malevolently.

"Smart hombre, ain't yuh?" the renegade snarled in an early-morning temper. "Your kind lives long—once in a while!" He was referring to Kip's extreme care not to disturb their sleep during the night.

"Lay off, Clabe," Blacky ordered lazily. "Get out there and start some grub if you're honing for something to do."

Glowering at Colerain as if he would like to take action on the spot, Tanner grudgingly complied.

When they were done eating an hour later they let him scrounge enough food to sustain some sort of an interest in life. Kip had quickly learned to ignore the brutal remarks tossed in his direction. As the morning advanced and the sun burned away the frosty chill, he gathered from their indolent lounging that, tense as they were under the rough surface, they were waiting for something. The enforced delay lasted throughout the day. First one and then another strolled up the slope of a nearby ridge to scan carefully the surrounding waste of mountains and canyons. But one of them always kept a baleful eye on Kip's slightest movement.

Although he continued to pick up fugitive information from their talk during the afternoon, scarcely a word was directed at himself save in revilement or contempt. They cared less than a snap of the fingers for him and as a result made no attempt to conceal the slightest detail of their plans. Their gradual revelation of the plot against Pat Stevens drew Kip's nerves tighter than ever, for he knew it was already too late to warn the Lazy Mare owner.

A second night and another day passed slowly, with escape no nearer than before. The third day was started as casually as ever by the renegades, who waited with the venomous patience of rattlers.

Midmorning passed calmly. An hour later, however, a faint hail dragged the men quickly to their feet. "Who's that coming?" Carnes demanded sharply.

"Who would it be?" Blacky was harsh. "We'll soon know how Durango made out!"

It was several moments before a rat-faced man rode into the grassy hollow, mounted on a tall claybank well calculated to catch the eye. It was Durango. His movements were curt as he reined in and looked them over glumly.

"Well, Durango! Is it war—or women?" Blacky bellowed with rough humor.

"If yuh mean did I rope them hombres, the answer is no," Durango snapped, glaring at Colerain malevolently. "I done my part, but Spink's too smart for us. Dang him, he balked!"

Blacky was alert in a flash. "He wouldn't follow yuh t' Palmer?" he demanded angrily.

"Dropped out after four or five miles. I had him and Gentry hooked and taking the line good. They must've smelled a rat."

"That's your fault, Durango!" Tanner yelled. "I warned yuh Helm would recognize that claybank! Any other bronc at all and you and Palmer'd have nailed them two—but no, it had to be that one! Take mighty good care of your own hide, and the hell with the rest of us!"

"Quit it, Clabe," Blacky snapped, thinking rapidly. "It was a good scheme—but we'll have to figure something else. We'll get back to Palmer and see what gives. Maybe we can pin the rap on Jack and Spink some other way."

"We better get about it then," flashed Carnes. "Those birds can still be grabbed; or we can comb 'em out of Stevens's range. But not while we're hanging here!"

Durango was sufficiently disgusted with his failure to agree readily to the suggestion of some further attempt. "Hump yourselves, then, and let's get goin'!" he cried impatiently.

Carnes and Tanner made a rush for their saddles, only to note that Blacky stood regarding young Colerain with sinister doubt. They delayed, angry determination in their set faces.

"What are yuh starin' at him for? Knock him off and be done with it!" demanded Clabe ruthlessly.

"Yeah." Carnes was even more chillingly deliberate. "He knows too much for his health. Or do I mean ours?"

"Well—" Blacky's expression failed to soften in the slightest. "No harm in given even a rabbit some part of a break." He stared at Kip. "All right, you. Leave!" He thumbed significantly across the rocky gully. There was no shred of doubt about the direction in which Colerain was to depart. "Jump, now—if you hope to make it!"

Kip stared back with ice stealing along his veins. He had watched this crisis coming for hours; now, suddenly, it was on him. Not for an instant did he suppose that they meant him to escape with his life. It was their cruel and merciless game to force him to run the gauntlet across the broken gully like an exposed, defenseless rabbit until he reached the point where their guns would inevitably cut him down.

The others caught on at once, spreading out and drawing their guns to insure a hand in the grim game. "Come on, cowpunch! Take off," blazed Tanner fiercely.

Like a condemned man Colerain strode slowly toward the gully. A single glance into the rocky depths made him shudder. It was rough and uneven enough down there to break the leg of a running man—and the cover was too scant to conceal his body for more than a minute or two from searching bullets.

He stood for long on the brink, delaying his start, that they grew angry. "Come on, come on! Get it over with." Clabe Tanner barged forward as if he would hurl Kip bodily over the edge.

Colerain eyed him desperately. "Don't crowd me," he threatened hoarsely. It suddenly struck him that if he could beguile Tanner within arm's reach there was just a ghost of a chance for him—though even then it would be nip and tuck.

"I'll kick yuh off," Clabe threatened wickedly, his stride quickening. The other owlhoots quickly saw what might happen. "Lay off, Clabe—stay away from him!" Blacky roared. Tanner might never have heard him.

"Blast you—git!" Tanner ducked as Colerain suddenly snatched up a rock and flung it in his face. He launched a savage kick but was totally unprepared for it when the puncher grabbed his leg and wrenched violently. With a squall of fury Clabe thudded to the ground, attempting a frantic defense with his arms as an unleashed wildcat leaped on top of him.

Colerain, intent solely on capturing the man's gun in the least possible space of time, succeeded with a harsh cry of triumph. A vicious clip with its barrel put the outlaw to sleep in a twinkling. Oblivious of thunderous gunfire and the slugs buzzing about him, Kip rose to his knees, the Colt in his fist bucking.

Jip Carnes yelled and ducked, and Durango whirled his valuable horse toward the cover of the cabin. Colerain blasted two shots at Blacky to halt his belligerent rush; and before the killers could concert their action, he dived over the rim of the gully and raced along under its edge.

A shot or two racketed, but he wasn't spotted. Fifty yards below, hearing the clap of furious voices as the renegades hastily reorganized their attack, Kip crawled out of the gully into the scant protection of scrub pine along its edge. The yells came now from the gully behind him, and rocks clattered. His pursuers were in full cry.

Grimly set on getting himself a horse, the puncher swiftly circled the little flat and raced through the pines. He saw no one as he halted briefly at the edge of the open. His horse was standing not far away. This was his chance.

With long strides Kip closed in on the startled bronc. The saddle had been stripped off, but he was able to grab the dangling bridle. Swinging astride bareback, he calmed the animal with a hand and turned it into the trees. A yard, three yards—it began to look as if he would make it.

There wasn't time to drive the other ponies off. In any event, there was still Durango's fast claybank to consider. His only real hope was to break trail as he went and throw the owlhoot off the scent as quickly as possible. Kip turned south, advancing quietly for a quarter mile; then he kicked the paint horse into its best pace and raced away.

10.

DESPITE AN EXCELLENT START, Colerain's luck was by no means as good as he had hoped. He was scarcely a mile from the old line camp when he received unmistakable evidence that his flight was discovered and he was being dogged. He had taken at once to the canyons with the object of losing his pursuers amidst the fallen timber and naked rock. Suddenly, as he worked his way through the bottom of a steep-walled chasm, a huge rock weighing many tons crashed down from above, smashing through crackling brush and leaping from shelf to bench down the dizzy slope with echoing thunder.

Though it had not even come close it set Kip's heart to thudding heavily. He abruptly wheeled and turned back up the canyon, using every means in his power to move quietly. He could see nothing as he gazed about him, yet half an hour later, while climbing toward a rocky gap that led to a yet wilder branch of the canyon, he heard the spang of a high-powered rifle. Rock fragments flew clattering about his head.

Colerain made the gap and was for the moment safe. But the fact offered no deceptive sense of security. "That's Durango on my trail," he muttered tensely. "He had a rifle on his saddle . . . How can I lose that wolf, with the horse he's got under him?"

More than once in the next couple of hours it looked as if he would not succeed. The rat-faced renegade clung persistently to his tracks, and the effort to throw him off drove Kip miles deeper into the Culebras.

Time and again he stole a moment from watching the

rough ground or his own back trail to glance anxiously at the westering sun. Inexorably the hours were passing, and Kip seemed farther than ever from carrying a warning to Stevens and the others about the owlhoots' new plans. Panic rose in him at the thought.

"I've got to shake off that leech, and make it fast!" he reflected tightly.

But he could not. The afternoon waned, finding him deep in the tumbled ridges and still dodging. Each time he tried to circle back his nemesis cut him off and turned him. Durango's object was to corner Colerain on the heights and finish him off; had he deliberately tried to bar his quarry from reaching Powder Valley he could not have planned better.

Kip watched the twilight grow and thicken with a feeling of disaster. He began to wonder all the more if he would ever come out of this alive. Only as darkness deepened under a star-spangled sky did he realize his personal liberation. Durango could not hope to track him now, and if the renegade took up the trail tomorrow morning he would be left hopelessly behind.

Setting his face resolutely eastward, Colerain started straight down the mountains. He was weary, his stomach empty. His bronc was in little better condition. He remedied this in part by halting at a canyon stream, allowing the animal to browse for twenty minutes and taking his own belt in a notch. Then he thrust on.

The sickle moon rose low over the towering range for a time, affording meager aid. When it sank the unrelieved blackness was intensified. Kip pushed doggedly on with increasing difficulty until, fearful of breaking his horse's legs on rocks concealed in the slash, he was forced at last to pull up.

Troubled sleep visited him fleetingly before he saw the first ghostly evidences of breaking dawn. Soon he was on his way once more. He saw no sign this morning of Durango, yet he did not spare himself. There were miles to cover still, and his concern for India Pickett and her mother grew with every minute.

There was a reasonable hope that they were safe and

unmolested; but he meant to take no chances now that he knew the malign forces unleashed on this mountain range. Hard as he drove himself, cursing his ineptitude for the delay, it was past midday by the time he pounded down into Coldwater Canyon and approached the Spade ranch buildings. He peered anxiously, but no one was in sight about the place. There was an ominous note in its silence and desertion.

Kip paused in the empty yard for no more than an agitated glance about. Then he slid to the ground and, whipping his Colt out, made for the door on the run. It was unbarred, giving without resistance to his powerful lunge.

"India! Mrs. Pickett!"

He burst inside, calling frantically. The response was instant and totally unexpected. A rough hand darted from the half-open door and snatched his gun from his grasp. At the same time a gun barrel slashed down on his head, effectively scattering his distracted wits and knocking him sprawling.

He lay for a moment inert, till a harsh voice shocked him back to full awareness. Turning with an effort, he looked backward and up. Jack Gentry and India were standing there, impellingly intent on each other, exchanging hot words.

"It was not necessary for you to do that!" the girl flashed, gesturing angrily toward Colerain. "If you must be told the truth, I care fully as much what happens to him as I ever will about you!"

"Nonsense! You may have that idea now." Gentry grabbed for her wrist, clamping an iron grip on it. "I'll undertake to persuade you different, girl!"

India struggled briefly and ineffectually, unable to break herself free. Kip understood in a flash what had occurred. All Gentry's oily wiles had failed with the girl, and now he had turned mean. In a rage the puncher attempted to struggle up and failed, slumping back down with a throbbing head and fainting senses.

"You'll never change my mind, Jack Gentry!" The girl's words rang with contempt and loathing. "Let go of me and take yourself off! I'm not at all anxious to ever see you again!"

Jack's laugh was harsh. "So I'm not good enough for you now, eh? Well, we're good enough for your ma—she's out riding somewheres with Spink now!"

Kip's thoughts whirled as he struggled weakly to a sitting position. Gentry's cutting words answered one of his questions; yet his keen concern for these women had not been wrong. Jack's raw craving for this girl had driven him over the line, and there was no telling what lawless course he would take now that he had had an unexpected opportunity.

Kip's torment forced him laboriously to his feet, and he propped himself against the wall. Jack, his ordinarily handsome face ugly, paused to watch him. "Decide to wake up, did yuh?"

Colerain glared across at him. "Take your hands off her, Gentry!" he panted through white lips.

Jack grinned, and the wide streak of sadism in him flashed to the fore. "Make me," he goaded. This was too much for India. Once more she attempted to tear herself loose. Gentry blocked her efforts tolerantly, if with a certain roughness.

"Make up your mind that I'm your boss," he jeered at her coolly. "It'll make things easier for us both—"

"What will you do with her?" Colerain jerked out, his eyes burning like coals. His strength was flowing back, but he still could not trust his legs.

"I'll make a man's woman of her, for one thing. She won't be interested in boys anymore, Colerain . . . Meanwhile, we'll take a ride for ourselves." A calculating note crept into Jack's voice. "If Spink can ride his girl around, I'll go him one better. We'll take a—wedding trip. That's it, by gorry! . . . Where's your hat?" He shot a bold look at the girl's averted face. "You'll need one—and a hanky or two, I suppose!"

Kip charged blindly away from the wall. Gentry shoved him easily aside, tripping him. Colerain's inability to cope with this strapping renegade was obvious. Tumbling sharply, he attempted without success to pull himself up.

Jack hauled India bodily into her room to oversee the

preparation of a small bundle. The girl had fallen silent and tense, fearfully watching his every move and gesture. She had long ago guessed what he probably was; and she knew the potentialities of his kind with the unfailing accuracy of feminine intuition.

"Come on—hurry it up!" Kip heard the man's rough admonition. "I'll argue this out with your ma if I have to. You'll think better of us both if I don't!"

He hustled India out of the house sternly while Colerain made a grim effort to struggle up. Gentry coldly kicked him back. Kip groaned his helplessness, conscious for a while of the sounds of Jack hastily getting up horses. These presently died out, and Kip knew with a sense of doom that the pair was gone.

Desperation at length drove him to action, though he knew there was no point in rushing about senselessly. Finding a liquor bottle which Madge Pickett kept on a shelf, he downed a slug. Then, battling impatience, he forced himself to hunt for food to stay a raging appetite. With a huge sandwich in his hand he burst out into the yard.

His bronc was gone. He had expected Gentry to haze it beyond reach, and he was not disappointed. But Kip knew, as the wily renegade did not, where the Pickett cow ponies grazed. Twenty minutes later, with renewed energy, Colerain jumped aboard a mare bareback and swung her head. Three minutes at the house sufficed to throw on a saddle and cinch it tight.

It was anybody's guess which way Jack was headed with the girl. Kip knew only that help was certain over at the Lazy Mare; moreover, he could deliver his belated warning there, on the off-chance of its usefulness. He dug his heels in and headed for Steven's ranch on the double.

When he had barely reached the fringe of Iron Ridge the young fellow hauled in abruptly at the sight of two riders bobbing along. He let out a yell, waving. To his intense relief if was Helm Spink and Madge Pickett who rode forward to meet him.

"Where in tunket have you been, boy?" Madge greeted him severely, her warrior's face drawn into lines of disfavor.

"Never mind that! I just came from the ranch, which is more to the point!" In tumbling words Colerain spilled out a brief version of what had taken place there. Spink listened with hardening face.

"Hold on, buster," he interrupted harshly, his eyes glinting dangerously. "Yuh can't mean that Gentry hauled that girl away with him—carried her off?"

"*I* couldn't stop him, mister!" Kip displayed his bruises. "Unless he was throwing a handsome scare into India, he sure as shooting abducted her!"

"Why, damn his impudent liver!" Spink raged. "So *that's* what he was buildin' up for! . . . I'll tear the fool's head off!"

There could be no mistaking his savage fury. Given his warmth of feeling toward Madge, his championing of the girl would be instant and fierce. Hauling his horse around, he would have burst hotly in pursuit on the dead run, had not Madge Pickett quickly crowded close to grab his bit chains and bring him to a stand.

"Just a minute, Helm—" She was as calmly masterful as he could have been. "Don't fly off the handle about this! I feel bad too about goin' to Pueblo when Indy needed me, but I don't aim to have my girl plumb in the way of flyin' lead while you two play your little game!"

Spink subsided unwillingly, his rocky face bleak. "Say what yuh got to say. We're wastin' time!" He did not knock her hand away from his bridle, however, as he might easily have done.

"First, where'll that weasel go?" she barked shrewdly.

He began a vehement reply, pausing to look quickly at Kip. "What did you hear, Colerain?"

Kip had gained the impression that the other man meant to ride far and fast. Spink nodded curtly. "Jack's nervy and likes to brag. He'll strike straight back for the Roost, or I'm crazy."

"Over the mountains—?" Madge had heard of Robber's Roost, though in no particular detail.

Helm nodded. "In Utah," he said simply and expressively.

Madge showed no dismay, however. Instead her face was a study in stiffening determination. "Drat the man! . . .

We'll go back to the ranch, Helm, and get a pack ready. This could be a long trip," she announced sturdily. "No use of you swearing, because I'm goin' along. I've fully made up my mind to that!"

Spink looked blankly at Colerain, then back at her.

"Hang it, Madge! You can't do that," he protested angrily. "It ain't safe in that country for a grown man!"

"No matter. I'll show those hyenas who's grown up if it comes to that! . . . Who's wastin' time now?" she countered tartly, her eyes flashing.

Spink opened his mouth, closed it again, and shrugged. Evidently he knew her too well to protest further. "Get going then, woman," he growled. "You'll have to stand a rough pace, remember that. We could overhaul that crawlin' rattler this side of the Colorado, and I aim to try!"

"Come on, Kip." The doughty woman had already started; but the puncher quickly spoke up.

"You two go on. We could use help—and I've got to see Pat Stevens right off. I'll catch up," Kip promised. "Somebody's got to watch Spade for us or it'll go to smash!"

His final argument was convincing. Neither attempted to halt him as he rode on toward the Lazy Mare, driving the pony hard to make up for lost time. Since Kip did not know what he might expect there it was a vast relief for him to find Stevens standing in the yard, talking to the lanky red-headed man everyone called Ezra. Both turned to gaze at him as he pounded up, the eager words already on the tip of his tongue.

"Well, Colerain!" Pat had asked Spink to send the young fellow over, never expecting anything to come of it. But here he was, and it was obvious that Kip bore a pressing message. "What's on your mind? Where have you been, anyhow?"

"Stevens, did you know a crowd of tough hombres have got designs on your cattle?" the puncher burst forth. "I learned that three days ago—but I couldn't get back!"

"Relieve your mind." Pat's smile was grim. "That game's already been tried, and the score is in." His eyes narrowed shrewdly. "You look as if you'd been treated rough—"

"I have." Kip related tersely how he had been grabbed and held on the range four nights ago. "You seem to know all I managed to learn—and a blame good thing, too. But that's only the start, Stevens!" In swift phrases he told what he had found on his return to Spade. The pair listened incredulously.

"I told yuh, Stevens," Ezra broke out gruffly at the end.

"It all ties up with Spink elopin' with that Pickett woman—"

"Elope nothing!" Colerain was sharp. He told about his meeting with Spink and Madge Pickett an hour since. "Mrs. Pickett wanted to do some shopping. Helm evidently persuaded her to make the trip to Pueblo and went along to squire her. They got back barely in time to start after Gentry . . . Whatever luck a woman of her age will have out there in the canyons!" he broke off in alarm. "Good as she means, she'll only slow Spink up . . . You've got to help me save that girl, Stevens!"

Pat was under no illusions concerning the menace of Jack Gentry. The man had reverted suddenly to savage lawlessness—and had done so while a Lazy Mare hand. It did not take the tall ranch owner long to make up his mind.

"Right, Kip. We'd better hop it! We'll need good broncs and a supply pack. I'll send a man for Sam, and we'll pick up Sparks and Hagen. This looks like a long haul through the hills. You can fill us in as we go."

Colerain would have protested these elaborate and time-consuming preparations. But Pat did not wait to hear him out, turning instead to swift action. He called orders, setting the machinery in motion for a start as soon as possible.

Pat had anticipated grief for India Pickett and her mother from the day of their arrival. And though this emergency had come suddenly, it was no surprise.

They threw packs together while Fred Sparks and his waspish partner rode in from the range. Johnson himself snared a stout roan out of the corral for Colerain, silently supplying a good rifle as well. By the time Sam Sloan came jogging up, bristling with importance at being included, all was in readiness.

"All right, boy!" Pat swung into the saddle, motioning to the puncher. "We'll make for Coldwater Canyon first and pick up the trail from there if we can. On the way over I want you to give me the lowdown about Spink's slant on this whole affair."

Without further ado they set off, half-a-dozen strong.

11.

To NO ONE'S SURPRISE, Spade ranch in Coldwater Canyon was found lonely and abandoned. A handful of Circle C Bar cows, grazing within sight of the log house, were the only signs of life.

Colerain was able to announce after a hasty reconnaissance that a supply pack had been thrown together in the kitchen. Tracks in the dusty yard showed that three horses had very recently pulled away. The answer was plain. Madge and Helm Spink had set off hurriedly with a pack animal in tow.

"What about her stock, Stevens?" the puncher asked worriedly. "I'm not staying, no matter what anyone says!"

Pat quickly relieved his anxiety. "Johnson's sending Candy Evans and Eph Sample over here tonight with orders to watch the place," he informed.

Paying no attention to this talk, Ezra made sure of the course Spink and Mrs. Pickett had taken. He turned then to give the others a disgusted glance. "What's the delay here?" he rumbled.

They thrust on, giving the tall redhead plenty of room to work. A tracker of parts, despite his loss of an eye, Ezra wasted little time in trailing the pair up the canyon for a considerable distance. Finally their sign climbed out of the canyon and struck into the hills. It was not difficult to determine before the afternoon wore away that Spink was making for a high pass in the Culebras.

No halt was made until darkness put an end to the lanky tracker's usefulness. They pitched camp in a scrub-grown hollow below timber line, with the brilliant stars hovering deceptively close overhead. The men found time while eating for a terse exchange of words.

"Ain't seen a thing of Gentry and that girl's tracks," pointed out Ezra gruffly. "Could be we're all makin' a mistake about him."

"Spink was absolutely sure Jack would head for the Roost," Colerain said vigorously. "Where else could he be sure India wouldn't tip the apple cart on him?"

Silence ensued while they thought it over soberly. It was Sam Sloan who finally spoke up. "Gentry knows he's got Spink to deal with," the chunky man said sagely. "He'd stay off the straight trail, at least till he'd got some mountains behind him. Could be he expects help at the Roost. I dunno where else he'd find any."

"How about that, Hagen?" Pat turned to the owlhoot. "Is there some other hideout that Gentry might possibly head for?"

Trap shook his head decidedly. "Jack comes from somewhere up north, Stevens, and he can't go back. He's well known in the Roost. He'll make a beeline for there, if for no other reason than to strut around."

Pat was strongly inclined to agree with this. From what Colerain said, moreover, he felt sure that Helm Spink saw things in the same light. In his deep concern about Madge's daughter the giant renegade had an impelling reason for not making any mistakes. It seemed likely he would read Gentry's mind more accurately than anyone else.

Kip Colerain was the first to stir the following morning. At this altitude the predawn air was freezing. The puncher got a blaze going and impatiently aroused the others. They ate hurriedly and were off long before the flashing sun, edging the level plains to the east, drew a line of gold across the tall peaks.

They wound down the long sweep of dense forest that led to the Isabels and the tumbled ranges beyond. Even the faint guide of Spink and Madge Pickett's trail was lost, however, as the way led over worn granite and through rocky canyons. Ezra turned to Pat.

"Take hours t' work out their sign," he observed briefly. "I can do it if yuh say so. We'll travel slower'n they do."

Colerain had already shown signs of chafing at the delay. "Skip it, Ezra," he exclaimed. "We know where we have to go. Let's get on with it!"

Pat signed his acquiescence, well aware of the young fellow's anxiety. "We'll have a better chance of picking up that pair if we shove right along," he announced.

It was all they needed. Drilling on at a mended pace, they dropped the miles behind. Another hard day saw them threading a devious course down the rugged west slope of the towering Rockies. For hours on end there had been no sign of life in this remote and lonely land. There would be none before they struck the notorious Owlhoot Trail, which etched the wild backbone of the West from the Hole in the Wall in northern Wyoming all the way to the Texas Panhandle, with many an offshoot and hidden pocket along the way.

"You boys know the Robber's Roost trail," Pat said bluntly to Hagen. "Put us on it just as soon as you can."

Trap had known for a matter of days that his past was no secret to this level-eyed man. From caution and wariness he and Sparks had advanced to reserved confidence. Their freedom of manner increased steadily as they drew near the outlaw country. Yet even now there remained a lingering doubt in their canny minds.

"We ain't none too welcome there at the Roost. Yuh must know that much, Stevens," Hagen volunteered now. "Spink has to be ahead of us. But *he* ain't the last word in there no more, either—"

Pat realized how his mind worked. "Suit yourself, Hagen. The risk you're running isn't a circumstance to ours. I'll do my best to back you up, of course. That's all I can promise."

Trap nodded. "Suits me. I'm backin' Spink myself. If a crack at Lant Palmer goes along with it, I'll take my chance and won't kick."

It was Stevens's private hope to overtake Spink before his rage at Jack Gentry's treachery drove him to some disastrous act. But the big outlaw was driving hard despite the handicap of a woman companion. The next day they turned into the Outlaw Trail in the high sagebrush country

MAN FROM ROBBER'S ROOST

of western Colorado. There they presently picked up the tracks of Spink's horses, which wound over the lonely swells into the unknown. Ezra judged that Helm and Madge Pickett were only a matter of hours ahead of them.

"Any signs at all of Gentry?" asked Kip urgently, trying to pin the lanky redhead down.

Ez shrugged. "Been some travel over this trail in the last day or two," he allowed. "It's anybody's guess who it was, boy. No use of my lyin'."

"Hang it! There can't be but blame few girls come this way," insisted the puncher discontentedly. "India'd have dropped a shred of ribbon or something, no matter how hard Jack tried to prevent her!"

"Keep your eyes open then," Ezra retorted, tired of this needling. "We're all after that girl, Colerain, or we wouldn't none of us be here."

Kip subsided uneasily. Thereafter he allowed nothing to escape his vigilant watch; and late that afternoon, as they jogged steadily north up the faint trail through the wilderness, it was his sharp eyes that spied a thin, hazy skein of smoke rising above the sagebrush far ahead.

Pat immediately called a brief halt while they conferred. "Somebody up ahead of us, that's sure," Sam Sloan declared. "Big mistake to take it for granted who. This country's some variously populated, in case yuh need remindin'."

With the possible exception of young Colerain, none of the men present were inclined to question his statement. All but him had come this way before and had ample cause to recall the experience with something less than enthusiasm.

"Must be a camp, with that fire goin'," Fred Sparks offered. "We taking a look, Stevens?"

Pat's nod was prompt. "I'm not missing a single bet. We'll play this one close to our vest, though. If it's anyone we don't know we'll draw off and push on our way."

This was a country of rolling brushy swells broken by red sandstone dykes and ledges which afforded ample cover. They rode on, turning off a quarter mile from the mysterious campfire and threading the hollows with care as they drew up. After a while they saw a number of booted figures moving about the blaze, beyond the obscuring sage. Evening was coming on as Pat ordered the horses left in a draw while they crawled on.

The brush rendered it comparatively easy to work up close enough to hear rough voices. No one doubted for a moment that they were looking at an outlaw camp. In this gloomy, silent and empty waste the renegades made no attempt at concealment. Yet Stevens gathered at once that some unusual tension agitated them, and that they were very much annoyed at one of the number.

"Don't give us no song and dance about your pals," one of them exclaimed harshly. "Yuh got no business showin' your face back here—!"

Pat, who crouched beside Ezra as they peered through the sage, felt the tall tracker nudge his arm. "Off there to the left," Ez breathed tensely. "It's that Pickett woman, standin' with her fists on her hips . . . Boy, them hombres've grabbed her and Spink!"

He was right. Madge herself left no doubt as she burst forth vigorously. "What do you care where Helm Spink goes or what he does?" She could command a roaring voice, and she turned it on now full blast, striding forward to confront the outlaw spokesman. "You got a gall, Cagle, if that's your name! There may be five of you here, or you wouldn't be half so brash. But Helm'll settle your hash, never fear!"

It was a gusty attempt at intimidation, but it failed. The man called Cagle thrust her roughly back. "Get away from me, you old battle-ax," he shouted. "Dang me if I know what Spink is thinkin' of, bringing the likes of you out here—unless he aims to hide behind your skirts!"

This drew a bellow of fury from Spink. He came charging out of the shadows to throw himself at Cagle with bitter indignation. Nearly as big as Helm himself and certainly not moved by fear, Cagle met his rush belligerently. They traded heavy blows, staggering about the fire till the other owlhoots closed in on Spink and hurled him back. Madge would have bit and clawed like a wildcat if she could have barged into the melee, but she was shouldered roughly aside.

MAN FROM ROBBER'S ROOST 91

"No use of you champin' the bit," Cagle yelled at Spink savagely. "You raised enough hell at the Roost, Spink! You ain't takin' this female tiger there nor you ain't goin' there yourself!"

Baffled and at bay, Helm crouched glaring. "Your case will be settled after I get there, Cagle!" he shouted back defiantly.

"Not before your own," snarled Cagle, hatred in his taut voice. "Palmer'll have some things to ask you! What became of Curly and Hank Taylor? Do you know? . . . Where's Blacky Nevers now, Spink? Are you ready to answer that one?"

"Not to you," Helm spat back. He was busily placating Madge Pickett's raging indignation and trying at the same time to lead her off.

After he had made sure no further violence was imminent, Pat slowly backed away, signing to the others to follow. It was dark enough now for them to stand erect, as long as they called no attention to their movements. "Bring up the horses," Pat instructed Kip quietly.

The puncher hastened to comply. Stevens waited till all were remounted, then led the way back to the beaten trail. "Follow my lead now—and let me do the talking," he warned in a low voice.

They clung to his heels as he jogged on boldly, coming presently in sight of the flickering campfire. There was a brief scurry there as the outlaws hastily drew out of the direct light, then silence.

"Who is that?" a harsh voice called sharply.

Pat quietly elbowed Hagen, who rode beside him. "That you, Cagle? . . . Sounds like you anyway," Trap answered gruffly.

There was a pause before Cagle answered, "What are you doin' here, Trap?" he demanded, striding forward. "Who is that with you?"

"Just some of the boys . . . Take it easy, can't you?"

Cagle watched narrowly as the newcomers moved up to the fire. He had never laid eyes on Pat or the partners or Colerain before; yet he was plainly distrustful. Least of all did he appear inclined to welcome Hagen himself. "What are yuh after?" he demanded flatly.

Pat glanced about with cool composure. "Where's Spink? I sure thought we'd overhaul him here—"

"I am here. Who's lookin' for me?" Helm's voice rumbled out of the dark. He came shambling close as bold as ever. Suddenly he halted. "You, Stevens?" For the moment he was at a loss. Obviously, whatever he thought was to come he had expected nothing like this.

Pat nodded to him casually. "Howdy, Helm. Hope you're able to tell us Jack is still okay—"

It was his cryptic way of warning the other of their real reason for being here. Spink nodded uncertainly. "He was last time I saw him." It was all the answer he chose to make within hearing of the hostile outlaws.

"That's something, anyway." Pat dismounted, cheerfully ignoring Cagle and his fellows, "Guess you won't mind our stopping with you?—Or maybe I should ask Madge," he added heartily, pointedly addressing his remarks to Spink.

"We mind plenty, friend—now yuh mention it!" Cagle threw in forcefully. "It happens we got business here, and it ain't yours!"

Pat pretended to misunderstand, winking broadly at Helm. "We heard the racket soon as we spotted your fire—I figured the boys were running a little charivari for you and the missus," he remarked indulgently. "No need for us to interrupt anything."

Spink stared at his enemies contemptuously, neither subscribing to Pat's fiction nor brushing it wholly aside. "They don't bother me."

Cagle glowered back. With the arrival of Stevens and his men, who obviously claimed casual cause with Spink, the scales were unexpectedly tipped against the outlaw in the matter of superior numbers. Cagle was hesitant to crowd the issue until reasonably sure of his ground.

"All right. If *we* don't bother you, then we'll squat," Pat answered the big fellow agreeably. Suiting his action to the words as if Cagle had not spoken, he gave orders for a meal to be got ready. Cagle's crowd watched huffily as the others calmly made themselves at home.

Spink clung close to the fire, unable to satisfy his mind

MAN FROM ROBBER'S ROOST

about Pat's deeper motives, yet realizing that his own safety lay in the fortunate appearance of these men. He and Pat made desultory talk totally unconnected with their real concerns, but from time to time they managed to convey an occasional hidden meaning by elaborate indirection. Stevens was not long in gathering that Helm had not yet seen Gentry or the girl. Although unable to learn for certain from Cagle, he believed the pair to have gone on ahead; and now the big man's single purpose, backed and abetted by Madge Pickett, was to ride in pursuit.

Cagle meanwhile had drawn his confederates aside. They were trying to figure out how to deal with this unexpected situation. Whatever their decision, they presently appeared bent on putting it into execution.

"Spink!" called one of their number, a burly cross-eyed individual named Galey. "Come here a minute. We want a word or two with yuh."

Helm barely turned his head. "Go on away," he growled angrily. "I ain't got a thing to say to you birds!"

"But this concerns Palmer," insisted Galey cajolingly. "Whatever you think of Cagle, mister, Lant sure won't like it if you get tough and refuse to listen—"

Spink gave no response whatever. Galey brazenly thrust close to the fire, trying to crowd him out like a puncher would cut a calf out of the herd.

"Are you comin'?" he demanded, cold menace in his voice.

Pat rode lithely to his feet, allowing the tin plate to slide from his knee. Fully aware of the threat of Cagle's men, who watched balefully in the shadowy light, he left no doubt in their minds of the cold resolve under his unruffled demeanor.

"Pull in your horns, you," he directed Galey curtly. "Spink happens to be boss here, if you haven't heard. I'll rock along with him!"

Cagle could stand no more, and he ran close. "You talk mighty big, Stevens—or whoever you are," he bellowed truculently. "We're siding with Palmer, and Lant don't want any part of Spink! From the looks of things that goes for you and the rest of your push!"

Pat turned to look him over deliberately. "Take your troubles to the Roost," he advised in a chilling tone, not in the least impressed. "That's where we're going. You can settle your business there, if that's how you want it."

Uneasy and stubborn, clearly outmaneuvered if not overwhelmingly outnumbered, the sullen outlaw delayed only a moment before turning away. Nobody listened to the surly retort he tossed over his shoulder. It was at least a momentary defeat for Cagle, and even his friends knew it.

12.

PAT AND HIS COMPANIONS made camp on one side of the fire, paying strict attention to their own affairs. Stevens anticipated no trouble overnight since Rufe Cagle had conspicuously drawn his men aside. Although their indolence and black looks said this was only an armed truce, it was one the outlaws found most convenient to themselves.

It was a restless sleep, with someone in either camp up and prowling about the better part of the night. In the early morning Madge Pickett emerged from her brush shelter to join the men. Stumping about efficiently, she soon had breakfast sizzling over the fire.

Cagle's crowd silently and sullenly attended to their own wants. Curiously enough, Kip Colerain was the only one to show nervousness at their presence. Pat understood that the young puncher's reaction was not the result of fear. Rather, Kip had hoped that Gentry and India might be swiftly overtaken in steady pursuit, and with the hostile owlhoots watching their every move this possibility dwindled.

When they had finished eating, the party prepared to move on. Cagle advanced boldly toward Stevens just before they started. "Shoving right ahead, are yuh? Take my advice, hombre, and turn back while yuh still can."

Pat looked at him coldly. "Who named you guardian of the Roost, Cagle?" he retorted.

The outlaw stared bitterly, struggling with the impulse to abandon all pretense of warning. "No use trying to tell you I'm thinkin' about that woman," he retorted sourly. "What happens to you and your pals will be sad enough—"

"Thanks for nothing, mister!" Madge chose to accept the barely veiled threat as an attack on her tough character. "Look after yourself, and you'll be doin' all right."

"Skip it, Rufe," Galey rejected the matter contemptuously. "We're goin' along with these birds whether they like it or not—and we won't miss a trick! I don't aim to have Palmer on my neck for the sake of a hard-boiled old biddy like her."

Spink was forced hastily to suppress the fuming Madge before she attacked the renegade bodily. Clearly she had no intention of taking any guff from these roughnecks. Cagle fell back, a baffled look on his face. Yet he remained stubborn.

"Let the tail go with the hide then," he burst out angrily. "But Spink's a traitor, whatever you make of him! He'll never get past the Roost, Stevens, nor you either!"

They thrust on at a deliberate pace, little more being said on either side. Pat was more than pleased at having come upon Spink and his companion; but at the same time Cagle's bitter defiance gave him considerable food for thought. It was a calculated part of his plan to back Helm unquestioningly before these hostile men, for the big owlhoot was their passport to Robber's Roost. He waited impatiently for an opportunity to talk to Spink in private; and this time the man would not be allowed to hedge and evade.

During the day his chance never came. They rode steadily on into wilder country, following the faint trail. The red cliffs and barren ranges gathered about them, falling away only to give place to increasingly forbidding scenery. Cagle's men clung close all the while, subjecting every member of the party to insolent scrutiny and constant surveillance.

By common consent there was no stop at noon, the time being spent in drilling on through the gloomy canyon approach to remote Green River. Daylight waned early in these confined gorges. They pulled up in late afternoon, finding a miniature park at the intersection of several canyons where there was sparse feed for the horses.

Firewood was scanty. On a sudden inspiration, Ezra

neatly solved the problem of at least partial privacy by coolly inviting the outlaws to supply the fuel for their own blaze. Galey was inclined to argue the matter, but Sam coldly shouldered him away from the tiny fire Colerain had got started, and the unwelcome men presently withdrew to a little distance where they pitched their own camp.

With this greater freedom for talk Kip could contain himself no longer. "We're not getting ahead at this rate, Stevens!" he burst out uneasily as they sat about over a frugal supper. "*Did* Gentry come this way? Is he ahead of us or isn't he? Does anybody know yet?"

In truth, they were all worried over India's predicament as time passed wholly unrewarded. "Take it easy, boy," broke in Spink, his glance stealing toward Madge Pickett. "Cagle can't be forced to tell us what we want to know. We might worm it out of him somehow with a little time—"

The others had various comments to make on the subject, but to little profit. Pat finally put an end to the discussion. "All of you keep your eyes and ears open," he warned. "The girl is our real object, and I don't want to waste time finding her. But don't breathe a word of what we're about if you expect any luck."

Helm appeared to concur in this, showing an unrest comparable to Kip's, if for different reasons. His face fell when Pat drew him aside as he was heading toward his blankets, but he delayed. The others rolled in, leaving the two of them hunched at the fire. To all appearances they were moodily indulging in a final smoke.

"Well, Spink." Pat's guarded tone was terse. "About time I knew just what we're stacking up against, isn't it?"

Helm's glance was cautious. "How's that, Stevens?" he parried.

"Put it this way. What's waiting for us there at the Roost?"

Helm stiffened, his big shoulders sagging. "Nothin' good, I expect." He appeared gloomy. "This Lant Palmer yuh hear so much about is the big augur—or things he is, anyhow. We was pards, more or less runnin' the outfit—before we fell out."

"Then he did run you and the boys out of there?"

Spink's grin was crestfallen. "Amounts to that, I reckon. We argued plenty. I never took it seriously till I found out he'd undercut me with the boys. I just never tried to block it—"

"How far has it gone, would you judge?"

"I ain't dead sure. Gentry and Trap and Sparksy stuck with me when Lant tried to force a showdown . . . These owlhoots are funny, Stevens. The crowd might've stood behind me if I'd shot it out then and there. I just wouldn't give Palmer that much satisfaction!"

Pat's face cleared. "Really, then, you pulled out to avoid a useless clash. Is that it?"

Spink assented grudgingly. "Not much use tryin' to persuade that bunch I wasn't playing yellow," he growled. "Lant Palmer was awful jealous of me. Probably he spread all kinds of stories—and I guess he *was* behind all those screwy doings in Powder Valley. Making dead sure I never came back!"

"What about Gentry?" asked Pat shrewdly. "He must be in about the same boat after siding you—"

Helm shook his head irritably. "Jack's an oily hombre," he reminded. "He'll talk Palmer around if he can get to him. I wouldn't put it past him to shove that girl in Lant's way in a pinch." His face darkened. "I don't know, Stevens. This'll be no bed of roses any way yuh look at it. But I aim to smash Gentry for that caper of his if I never do anything else!"

"You may have to smash Palmer before you can reach Jack," was Pat's curt summing up. "We're with you, if only for the sake of India and her mother. I can't promise you anything further, Spink. We have to go back and face the law," he reminded. "whether you do or not."

"You're doing fine," Helm caught him up quickly. "No man could ask for more. This deal Palmer handed me is beginning to get under my own skin finally. I won't expect no help when it comes to dealin' with him or Gentry personal."

Clearly he felt bitterly that Jack Gentry had flagrantly double-crossed him in abducting India Pickett, and Pat was content to let the matter rest there. Anything further the

MAN FROM ROBBER'S ROOST 99

developing situation might lead to could safely be left to the girl's mother, who surely had enough experience of the world to know exactly what she was doing.

Cagle and his followers were watchfully alert the next morning. A start was made in silence, and the party pushed on through the canyons.

It interested Pat a great deal to observe that Sam was fraternizing affably with the outlaws. Given his disreputable appearance and his fleshy jowls bushed with blue-black stubble, the stocky little man was able to convey a genuine impression of being one of them. Galey at least welcomed Sloan's attentions, probably with the object of picking up stray information about Spink's party.

Regardless of the outlaw's success or failure, Sam speedily demonstrated his ability to make progress on his own account. He seized the opportunity for a hurried word with Stevens while they were splashing across a treacherous canyon creek.

"Gentry's shoved on up the trail, Stevens," he muttered, crowding his bronc up alongside Pat's. "From what I could gather he must be a good half day ahead of us—"

"Good man," returned Pat swiftly. "At least we know we're on the right track."

"What was that, Stevens?" Cagle barked, coming up behind them unexpectedly, his tone and manner alert.

"If it's any of your concern," retorted Pat over his shoulder, "I was questioning whether we're on the right track to the Roost." His look was challenging. "Not that I think you boys would try to lead us astray!"

Though thoroughly deceived, the renegade became angry. "Don't kid yourself," he jeered harshly. "You asked for this, Stevens! We'll get yuh there fast, so don't worry."

It was almost an hour before Pat was able safely to pass Sam's information on to the others. Madge Pickett only nodded, a dangerous glint in her eyes. But Colerain received the ominous news with agitation. The certainty that Gentry was hurrying the girl on to the notorious outlaw camp made him doubly impatient.

"Can't we shove along faster?" he exclaimed, cruelly tortured by every moment's delay.

Madge impulsively reined over beside him, patting one

of his hands with motherly solicitude. "Never you mind, Kip," she advised gruffly. "There's surely no help for this—and we *are* getting along, son. If it should happen to rain India ain't made of sugar," she reminded practically.

But this was scant comfort to the distraught puncher. He had not the older woman's tempered self-control as a bulwark against his dread. Crowding to the fore, Kip succeeded in setting a somewhat mended pace, though he managed little more than putting the horses in a lather.

They made camp that night in the awe-inspiring depths of the spectacular Green River gorge. The river gurgled and slid sullenly over shallow rocks which made a practicable ford. Driftwood from the faraway Wind River range burned green-hued on their campfire. It was a chilly camp, the raw wind droning through the great canyon and eddying into the granitic overhang under which they took refuge.

Even Madge Pickett was blue with the cold in the dismal gray of the dawn. No time was lost in downing a steaming breakfast and shoving off on the long climb up out of the depths. It was midmorning before they emerged once more into the sunlight. Still the trail wound upwards through rocky, desolate wastes.

They came out in early afternoon on an area of high, rounded stone caps, which were sun-blasted and worn by water. Only low, gnarled cedar trees dotted the rough crevices, the cloudless blue sky arching down over a world of naked rock. Pat realized that they were rapidly nearing Robber's Roost from the cocky way Cagle and his cronies now thrust on in the lead. Madge Pickett clung close to Spink's side as the big outlaw rode moodily on.

"We'll soon learn what kind of a place this is," Pat murmured to Ezra and Sam. "We may not spot that girl right off. Keep your eye on everything in sight and don't miss a trick."

The Roost itself they found perched boldly on top of this lofty, desolate plateau. Avoiding the exposed crowns of granite and gneiss, the outlaws had erected their rendezvous amidst a maze of rocky dells that were scattered about with cedar and bristled with overhanging ledges. Coming out on a high swell above this extensive depression, they looked down on a veritable village. The camps

MAN FROM ROBBER'S ROOST   101

scattered haphazardly through the dells surrounded what was obviously the main camp.

"There's a shack yonder—" Ezra pointed out a sagging corner of its roof visible beyond the rocks.

Spink heard him, nodding. "It's the saloon," he supplied, "with a kind of hotel tacked on the end. Not much else up here to amuse the boys . . . Sort of a headquarters, yuh might say, where Palmer and his pals are apt to hang out."

Stevens knew enough about the easy organization of outlaw life to guide him as he rode boldly down into the protecting dells in search of a likely camp site. They found a spot conveniently on the fringe of the encampment, yet not so isolated as to excite particular notice. Sparks and Trap Hagen clung close to the others after the disappearance of Cagle and his fellows. Like Spink, they were restlessly awaiting what would follow when Lant Palmer learned of their arrival; but unlike him, they could not altogether conceal their nervousness as to the upshot.

Pitching camp, they settled down as if there was little on their minds. An hour passed, and nothing whatever happened. From time to time a strange owlhoot passed by their hollow with only an inquiring glance, and no one offered either greeting or challenge. Madge was by no means sure she liked this. The pointed way in which they were ignored seemed almost contemptuous. Plainly the word had gone forth.

Toward dusk Sparks and Hagen could stand it no more and decided on a bold move of their own. After a muttered conference with Spink they moved off. They were gone for an hour when Trap came hurrying back to camp breathless, his face mottled with sharply suppressed feeling.

"Fred's gone," he announced, his voice hoarse with tragic finality. "He was bound to push into that saloon! Durango picked a quarrel with him . . . and Sparksy got shot—tossed out of the bar like an old sack!"

Pat listened tensely. Gunfire had been heard about the camp from time to time; it might mean anything or nothing. This was obviously the first move in a siege that was bound to end in further bloodletting.

"That does it. No more wandering," he ruled decisively. "We'll stick to camp and let trouble come to us, if that's the way it has to be."

They did not have long to wait. Toward nine o'clock Sam Sloan moved back from the mouth of the hollow where he had been maintaining a watch. "Company comin'," he announced.

They heard the scuff of boots, and four spurred and armed men tramped forward in a close group to halt directly across the fire. Pat found himself gazing narrowly at a fish-eyed, flat-cheeked man whose authoritative mien marked him as Lant Palmer. The fellow's wicked glance raked them all and came to rest on Spink.

"Come back, have yuh."

The flat phrase was hardly a question. Helm's nod was stoic. "Here I am, Palmer. And what of it?" he retorted sharply.

The outlaw leader shrugged. Clearly he was using this opportunity to examine Spink's reinforcements, and those dull, beady eyes were not omitting a single detail. "You don't need tellin'," he said finally. "It's open range all around here, mister. Create a disturbance and you'll get what Sparks got!"

"Yes," rejoined Helm stolidly, moving deliberately to shield Madge Pickett. "There's Fred. We'll have to remember him. Shouldn't wonder if Blacky'd like a word with yuh about now, too!"

The shaft told. Palmer had dispatched Blacky Nevers on the ill-starred trip from which he would not soon return. But Lant only grunted. "He knowed what he was going up against. And so do you, Spink. This is the only warning you'll get!"

"Did Gentry tell yuh to say that?" Trap Hagen thrust in wickedly.

Palmer slowly turned his leaden glance on the other. "Mind your lip, Trap," he advised dourly. "And don't none of yuh bother to ask me for information—"

"You'll get about as much yourself, Palmer—before it's too late to do anything about it." Pat spoke up coolly. "I never met you, but from what I've seen so far I didn't miss a thing!"

The outlaw chieftain absorbed this taunt with stubborn

calm. He had no more to say. Making a sign to his lieutenants he stumped heavily off, leaving behind him no sense of relief at his departure, but rather a sense of growing menace.

13.

PAT ISSUED STRICT ORDERS that, without exception, no one was to leave camp that night, and a guard was posted. Ezra took the first trick.

"According to Helm this Lant Palmer is a snaky one," Pat told him. "So you can expect anything. Give us ten seconds' warning, and we'll be ready for it."

Sam grinned sardonically at his partner. "He'll stay awake," he promised. "Or I'll hand him a lily!"

Despite Colerain's worst expectations, however, no disturbance of any kind marred the night. The sounds of revelry finally died out toward the center of the big camp during the small hours, and dead silence followed. It lasted until it was broken by the chunk of an ax, and the acrid scent of wood fires tainted the frigid morning air.

Pat looked preoccupied as he ate breakfast.

"Looks like we're caught in a cleft stick, Stevens," Trap Hagen said. "Don't fool yourself that Palmer ain't havin' us watched like a hawk. I ain't forgettin' Sparksy—but you're the boss. What's our first move?"

"First off, we'll have to locate Gentry—and if possible, India," Pat answered thoughtfully. "I don't know just how far it's possible to get, but we'll make a try."

Trap grunted. "Well, take it real easy," he cautioned. "Fred thought he could bull his way through. You see where he wound up!"

Pat assented. "One or two of us can scout around," he pondered, "while the rest do a lot of loafing right here in camp where we'll look innocent."

Spink, Ezra and his chunky partner were listening to this

talk when Madge Pickett appeared from her sheltered corner of the rocks in time to overhear the closing words. She sniffed. "You'll have to draw lots for second chance, then," she tossed out.

Helm scowled. "How's that, Madge?" He had already grown critical of her during the long trip; yet he accorded her ungrudging respect as an individual with a mind of her own.

"Young Kip's been up and gone for twenty minutes," she informed them. *"He's* not letting any grass grow under his feet!" Her slightly scornful inference was plain. From the moment of her arrival at Robber's Roost she had vehemently professed not to understand the delay. In her mind the proper course was to locate her daughter directly and without wasting another minute.

"Just let me reach her, is all," she snapped. "I'll have a word for that Jack Gentry, too. See if I don't!"

The men looked pained. Sam Sloan had established a cordial if impromptu understanding with the plucky woman during the last day or so, but even his faint smile was weary now. "We may never hear what did happen t' Colerain if he goes bargin' around this place," said Sam plainly.

"Nonsense! I'll grant the boy don't belong among a bunch of roughnecks. All the same, I'll wager he learns more in short order than the rest of you put together."

Though obliged to acknowledge her staunch faith, Pat was not ready to leave the matter there. "You better shove off, Ezra," he told the tall tracker. "Bring Colerain back here if you can find him. I won't have him or anyone going off half-cocked . . . And I needn't tell you to keep your eye peeled and your ears open."

The big redhead left at once, but he did not locate Kip; and Ez was still absent when the object of his search came dejectedly into camp alone an hour after sunrise.

"Where've you been, boy? Did you learn anything at all?" Pat was sharp with him.

Kip shook his head. "Nary a thing, Stevens. I started out to circle this place, scouting from the humps. I must have walked two or three miles—climbing half the time—and I didn't see a thing to interest us. It was all wasted effort!"

"Humph!" Spink's response was curt. "What was the object of runnin' all that risk for nothing?"

"It wasn't for nothing! It was for India!" Colerain burst out hotly. "I had an idea Gentry might be holding her in a private camp separated from all these rowdies." Then his tone fell and his troubled face became a picture of gloom. "I guess I was wrong, I never found it."

"Did you cover the ground real good?" pressed Pat.

Kip spread his hands. "I combed this whole plateau and looked down every crack and gully in it! If India's here at all," he finished, "she's right here in this camp!"

"Kip, don't you do a crazy thing like that again." Madge was insistent. "We'll find Indy somehow. Let those men do it. If something happens to you too, I declare I don't know what I'll do!" Her concern for him was genuine and far different from anything she allowed herself to feel for the others, though Colerain was too distracted to take her solicitude at its full value.

"Something's got to be done fast!" he continued doggedly. "How do we know Gentry won't drag India away from this place once he's tipped off we're here? If that happens, we'll never find her!"

"No matter. From now on you'll stay put," Pat told him bluntly. "We all will, till Ezra comes back."

But the big redhead failed to put in an appearance. There was no indication of where he had gone or what he was up to, and their apprehension mounted with passing time. It was Sam who broke the waiting silence in midmorning with an exasperted growl. "We may be makin' a big mistake, Stevens," he declared uneasily. "It can't be no great secret why we're here. Fred Sparks likely got knocked off in that hotel because he learned too much. The same thing could happen to Ez—and how'll we know?"

"That's dead right. Durango knows us," Kip piped up. "He spent a whole day trying to down me—and Hagen says he's here in the Roost."

Pat was obliged to concede that things looked bad. If Lant Palmer so chose, he had only to immobilize them as he was doing now and pick them off one at a time. But before any decision could be reached in the face of this crisis Ezra himself came shambling into camp, sober and inscrutable as always.

"What happened, Ezra? What did you find out?" demanded Pat tersely.

Ez spread his long bony fingers. "Not much. Reckon I'll qualify as a guide to the Roost now—all except the inside of that hotel." His tone was apologetic. "It's safe enough out in the open. But that place looks too much like a bear trap to me!"

Kip's groan added eloquence to the serious faces about him. "Then we're no nearer to locating India than ever! Hang it, Ezra—"

"Well, I did get a line on Gentry anyhow," the big man said shortly. "Saw him postin' into that saloon big as life. I was afraid there was too many of his pals in there."

The words instantly electrified Spink. "Yuh say Gentry's in that bar now? That's all I need to know!" The huge outlaw turned on his heel and was sternly on his way when Pat quickly stopped him.

"Just a minute, Spink. Has it struck you that Gentry could be the bait to lure you into a trap?"

"Let it snap!" was Spink's harsh response. "I'm mad enough right now to fight a bear trap. Gentry'll think *he's* caught in one, I can promise yuh that!"

Pat knew the uselessness of trying to stop the man when he was in this mood. He thought swiftly. "All right. Gentry's got to be reached, of course. I'll go with you."

He warned Sam and Ezra to guard the camp and swung away beside Spink. They were startled as they strode through the rock dells to note how elaborate this place was. Camps had recently been pitched everywhere, while others had obviously been recently vacated. It was clear that countless roving owlhoots used this convenient hideout, coming and going at will. And it was equally obvious that the organization of the Roost was extremely free except for such authority as the boss of the hour was able to exert.

Pat glimpsed over forty or fifty men as he and Helm struck straight toward the ramshackle hotel. A few paused to stare after them, and a small group broke off talking to watch; but no one attempted to halt their progress. There was an open space not unlike a village square about the weathered, log-and-tarpaper hotel. Half-a-dozen saddle horses stood at the rack, but no men were in sight until a tall gangling figure moved into view around the corner of the building. Pat tightened up as he saw that it was Lant Palmer.

The outlaw leader spotted them instantly. His eyes went steely at sight of Spink. He moved slowly out to confront them, both hands a matter of inches from his low-slung guns.

"What's the idea of wanderin' around?" he bit off with sour emphasis. "You kissed this place good-by, Spink, when you pulled away from here."

Helm's mouth drew thin. "Stand aside, Lant." Palmer was directly between him and the entrance to the bar. Knowing as they did that Gentry was inside, this could hardly be interpreted as an accident.

Instead of complying the outlaw only lifted his rasping voice. "Yuh ain't wanted here. Go back!"

Stern as he was, he had sufficient respect for Spink's prowess to keep his eyes glued to the big man's face.

Suddenly, without Palmer's knowing just how it occurred, Pat was at his side. His hand fell on the outlaw leader's tensed wrist, and Lant sensed the iron lurking under that light touch.

"Easy does it, Palmer." Pat's tone was soft. "You and me'll stand here and talk while Helm steps inside for a drink." His smile was grim. "Breathe deep, old man. Nobody's going to get hurt—unless it happens to you. By accident, that is."

Braced thus by a man fully as reckless as himself, Palmer's face turned dark. His wicked glance switched to Stevens, and he seemed oblivious of Spink stepping coolly around him and walking ominously toward the saloon.

"Stevens, is it?" Lant's tense voice grated like a file. "What's your stake in this, hombre?"

"I just admire fair play all around," Pat retorted lightly, his faculties sharply alert. Aware that Spink had stepped into the bar, he waited for the flat pound of gunfire. Seconds dragged by, and nothing of the kind occurred. It was impossible to suppose Gentry was no longer there;

with half his attention, Pat had unmistakably caught Jack's loud hail when Helm thrust in the door.

Palmer was making a stout effort to cover his backdown. "Never seen you before, Stevens. Take some good advice and pull out pronto. You might down a man or two in here, but you'd never make it out. Spink can't see that."

"He hasn't got me in his pocket," retorted Pat smoothly. "Don't you try it either, friend. Just let me figure it out for myself."

He stalled the man along, half attentively. Spink had been in the bar for some minutes now, and still nothing had happened. Perhaps he was delaying to wring India's whereabouts out of Gentry before blasting the man. Meanwhile it was a touchy job holding this tough outlaw potentate at bay. At any moment Lant might make up his mind to try conclusions with his guns. To distract his mind Pat kept the talk alive.

Three owlhoots suddenly appeared, moving toward them. To all intents Pat and their leader were standing in casual conversation; yet their intent looks were curious. "Stall them off, Palmer." Pat's low order was insistent. "Or I won't answer for what happens!"

The three hailed Lant, who hesitated momentarily before waving them away. Pat's breath came more freely as he watched them stroll on from the corner of his eye.

It seemed a long time but must have been only a matter of moments before Helm Spink came striding out of the saloon. He nodded stolidly to Pat, barely pausing as he passed. "Okay, Stevens. Turn him loose." He was half contemptuous. "I'll soon put the Indian sign on him!"

Pat was instantly struck by this strange assurance. Abandoning Palmer with a brusque nod, he joined the giant as they set off for their camp. "Give it to me, Spink." He was frankly puzzled and surprised by the unexpected change in the other's manner. "I thought you went in there to tear the place apart!"

Helm waved a hand. "That's all changed now, Stevens." He seemed reinvigorated, his deep-set eyes flashing. "The plan's different now. Gentry explained a lot of things—and we aim to build a fire under Lant Palmer that will soon be too hot for him!"

Pat's lips parted. "How will you manage that?" he asked, more than half inclined to doubt what he was hearing.

"Well, it's a matter of politics—not easy to explain. There's been some changes here since we pulled out— Palmer ain't so strong. Jack's managed to get a fresh grip, and he thinks we can put the skids under Lant. It'll land me on top again."

Stifling his dismay, Pat saw only that with a smooth approach Gentry had actually talked the big outlaw out of his burning thirst for vengeance. He sparred for time to deal with this inexplicable development by pretending not to wholly understand, and Spink was still volubly explaining when they reached camp. Noting their arrival, the others alerted at once.

"What happened, Spink?" demanded Kip. "Did you smash that rat like you said you would—?"

Helm started to tell about his meeting with Gentry and their privately concerted plans to depose Palmer and take charge of the Roost. It was impossible to miss his triumph as he talked! He seemed utterly oblivious of the full meaning of his words for them.

"Did you find my girl?" Madge Pickett broke in on him harshly.

Helm broke off to stare at her, chagrined. "Hanged if I didn't plumb forget to ask that!" he confessed shamefacedly. "Gentry swore she was fine, and I figured we'd pick her up first thing—"

"Helm Spink, you're no better than a child, and a great fool to boot!" Madge pitched into him furiously. "Forgot to ask indeed! . . . I suppose you brought me all those miles to take charge of this damned Roost!" While he gazed at her with dropped jaw she continued to berate him soundly, leaving no possible question of her contemptuous scorn.

Her tirade left them all momentarily stunned, and they stared after her uncomprehending as she flounced away, her head tossing.

"Hold on there! Where you goin', ma'am?" Ez called finally.

Madge did not deign to reply, and they exchanged swift

MAN FROM ROBBER'S ROOST 111

glances in thoroughly cowed concern. "There'll be hell to pay if she barges in that hotel," Spink groaned, abruptly awakening to the enormity of his actions. "She heard me say Jack's over there—"

"Let's go." Pat made up his mind without hesitation. "I'm certainly not inclined to get in her way right now; but we can make ourselves handy if we're needed—which isn't exactly impossible."

They trooped toward the center of the camp, barely keeping Madge Pickett in sight. As they expected, she made straight for the hotel, avoiding the bar and heading for the main entrance. Even as they watched, a man tried to bar her way. Solidly built as she was, she sent him staggering aside.

Madge disappeared, and the watchers halted at a distance in alarm and awe. In no time at all it was obvious that things were happening inside the tumbledown hotel. They heard bangs, thumps and strident voices. Others noted the disturbance, and several owlhoots peered guardedly from the door of the bar.

Suddenly a man burst hurriedly out of the hotel in considerable disarray. He was followed by a second, more defiant figure, whom they saw at once to be Jack Gentry. Madge appeared in the doorway behind him, competently waving the twig broom with which she had forced their hasty retreat. "And don't you come back here again, you Gentry!" she bawled. "Or you'll be sorry for it!"

Colerain's breath sucked in as he caught a fleeting glimpse of India behind her mother's ample form. "Thank God! She found her," he choked. "I guess she can be trusted to look after her, too—"

Obviously Madge thought the same. As Gentry banged disgustedly into the bar, leaving the field to her, she caught sight of her own party. But she only had eyes for Spink, with whom she was obviously still furious.

"Don't you come near me, Helm Spink," she warned, "without an explanation! It'll have to be better than anything I've heard out of you yet, and don't you forget that neither!"

14.

AT THE FIRST PROMISE of unusual excitement outlaws had begun to gather outside the hotel from a dozen directions. They were a motley crew, rough and unkempt, few having known anything but a hard life. At their appearance Pat and his companions fell back to avoid a brush. Spink, however, refused flatly to go beyond earshot.

"If these buzzards get any notion of givin' Madge a tough time, I aim to be handy," he announced.

Yet the owlhoots appeared intent on no more than learning what had gone on. Some of them hurried into the bar, to emerge after a time guffawing uproariously. They passed the joke on with considerable zest. Evidently Gentry, having retired to the saloon after his ejection from the hotel, was saving face by retailing a facetious version of his experience.

Ten minutes later a man who appeared to wield some authority walked up to the closed hotel door and banged on it. After a delay punctuated with persistent knocking the door abruptly swung back and Madge Pickett filled the frame. A belligerent figure with her hands on her hips, she demanded loudly what this annoyance meant.

The fellow talked fast, aiming to appease her anger. But Madge was not to be cajoled. Suddenly she grabbed up the handy broom and brandished it vigorously. Her tormentor scuttled away amidst the jeers and catcalls of the watchers.

The door slammed, with India and her mother still securely entrenched behind stout walls. Pat watched the discomfited hotel man argue with one of Palmer's burly lieutenants, who shrugged and turned away. The tickled outlaws were laughing once more as a bottle from the bar circulated freely among them.

"Madge is pretty cute at that," remarked Sam shrewdly. "She knows them owlhoots'll let her get away with this if only for the yak they get out of it. Yuh needn't worry none, Colerain. Nobody'll get to that girl without fightin' past an uncommonly rough wildcat first!"

Such sage reassurance as this had its effect on Spink as well. "I sure hope you're right, Sloan." He sighed heavily. "Madge's gone plumb cold on me—but I got her into this. I won't throw her down, no matter what she says."

Since more curious outlaws had gathered and a night of hilarity appeared in prospect, they retired on Ezra's advice to their camp. It seemed singularly dull there in Madge's absence, and more than one of them noted it. Stevens, however, was concentrating on more serious problems.

"I suppose you know just how slim this leaves any chance of escape," he told Helm. "Those men will keep tabs on every move the girl and her mother make from now on. I gather Gentry had India hid in that place and was trying to keep it quiet. But not any longer. And that means our own chances of reaching those women have just about ceased to exist."

Colerain received the announcement with dismay. "Hang it, Stevens! Madge Pickett'll let *us* in—me anyway," he exclaimed with no more than forlorn hope.

"Oh, yes—once you fight your way through these owlhoots. You might make it with a platoon of cavalry," Pat said bluntly.

"Slack off, Stevens." Ezra pretended disgust. "We got to get in touch with 'em some way, o' course. The question is, how?"

None of them had any practical suggestion to make. The truth was, the same question in somewhat different form bothered Madge Pickett as time passed and she and her daughter found themselves completely isolated in this ramshackle four-room excuse for a hotel.

"Just calm yourself, girl," she told India severely for the third time. "You've got me with you, which is more than you had any reason to expect! If Jack Gentry or any other man tries to sneak in here I swear I'll bash his brains out. I mean it!''

The girl had expressed her violent loathing for her abductor and her urgent wish never to lay eyes on him again. But she was by no means as firmly convinced as her mother pretended to be that this wish would come about.

"Mother, sooner or later you'll have to face those men," she pointed out. "Difficult as it will certainly be, we can't avoid it."

Madge sniffed. "Forgetting something, ain't you?" Whatever her private thought, she chose not to confess any doubts. "Kip Colerain is out there, planning hard for your safety and nothing else. Pat Stevens too. And that Ezra and Sam are both good men in spite of their looks." She studiously avoided any mention of Helm Spink.

But India's dread of Gentry had sunk deep, and not without reason. Before the next day was well advanced he was already making an attempt to communicate with her.

There was plenty of food for Madge and the girl in the cluttered kitchen of the hotel, but water proved to be another matter. Usually, since there were plenty of hands available at need, it was carried in with buckets; and the embattled woman soon found that she had unintentionally closed this source of supply by barring the door to all.

She solved the problem with characteristic decision by stumping outside and peremptorily ordering the first man she saw to bring her a bucket. After the first jolt of surprise the owlhoot readily acquiesced, grinning. He ran all the way to the spring on the edge of camp and returned just as quickly. Madge coolly relieved him of his slopping bucket and slammed the door in his leering face.

An hour later, deciding to replenish her swiftly dwindling water supply, she calmly repeated the maneuver. The outlaws went along with this brand of effrontery, which they were forced to admire, and, winking and nudging, they presented themselves with a bountiful amount.

Masterfully accepting two of the buckets, Madge nodded to India to take the third. She had turned her back for a bare moment and noticed nothing. But almost at once after closing the door firmly she observed the girl surreptitiously tossing something into the fireplace. India's face was cold and set, and her mother was alert in a twinkling.

"What are you burning up, Indy?" She snatched the crumpled scrap of paper before it started to blaze. "Hunh!" Her grim face was a study as she smoothed it out. "Why, this is a note from Gentry. The gall of him! . . . That man handed it to you with the bucket."

"I didn't look at it," India spoke up hurriedly.

"I should think not!" But Madge made no bones about having her own look, and her eyes hardened as she read. *How far do you think you'll get without me?* the scrawl said. "Why, that impudent lickspittle!" She snorted angrily, glancing at the girl's face. *"When can I see you,"* she read accusingly. "Let's hope you don't have any such intention!"

"Mother, I can't help what he writes." India pinched back the angry tears. "I don't want to know what it says, and certainly I have no idea of doing what he says!"

"Well, really! I guess not." Madge snorted again, her square face in a thunderous frown. But she was satisfied. No more was said on the subject then, but India noted that during the day her mother began peering guardedly from the unwashed windows as if waiting for something.

Madge was quite sure Gentry would not give up with a single feeble effort, and at the same time she wondered what was being done to help them. She had tried to convey to Spink that nothing less than decisive action would be acceptable, and with her impatient nature she began promptly to watch for results.

It finally dawned on her that she might have a long time to wait. The long day dragged by dully, and nothing whatever happened. Watching the lazy activities of this camp soon bored her, but night was worse. It was the time the treacherous Gentry would be sure to pick for his sortie.

She stowed India comfortably in the cleanest and tightest room. Hours passed to the muffled laughter and talk from the bar beyond the stout log wall, and Madge dozed fitfully before the fire. Despite her courage she was uneasy, being far from blind to the problem which vitally concerned Pat Stevens. Though she and India were safe for the moment due to the whim of unpredictable men, how were they to get out of this ghastly trap?

Toward morning, in the midst of deathly stillness, Madge started awake to the scurrying of a mouse. *Or was it?* Taut and dismayed, the woman came heavily to her feet, listening keenly. There it was again! She peered fruitlessly from the windows into pitch darkness, then stole soundlessly to the door of India's room. The guarded murmur of voices coming from within froze her to the marrow.

Madge lunged furiously through and clamped a death grip on the shadowy form by the half-open window. It was not India. Something vaguely familiar in the sinewy shoulders gave her pause. "Who are you?" she hissed savagely.

"It's me—Kip," was the instant answer. "I slipped in to speak to India, Mrs. Pickett." Colerain was apologetic and plainly worried by his exploit.

Madge forced the window shut, then released a long breath. "You young scatterbrain," she berated him in a lowered voice. "Don't you know any better than to run such awful risks?"

"Well, sure. But I wanted—wanted to—"

"Did anyone see you coming in here?" she cut him off imperiously. Embarrassment was added to Kip's confusion at the penetrating question.

"I—had to slug one hombre out there. *He'll* never know how it happened," he confessed quickly. At these words India moved close to him, her grave concern plain.

"Kip! You shouldn't have—but I'm glad you did." She had many questions to ask, and though Madge's face softened in the gloom at the sound of their murmuring she was unable to remain in the background for longer than a minute.

"If you're able to get here why didn't that—Stevens come with you, boy?" she demanded irritably. It was Spink she missed, and she was trying to get Kip to mention him first.

"Pat would have turned thumbs down if he knew I meant to try." Kip explained about the tentative deal on the fire to take over the Roost and oust Palmer and his cohorts. "If that goes through you can walk out of here scot-free."

MAN FROM ROBBER'S ROOST 117

"What's holding it up then?" Madge snapped shrewdly.

Colerain hesitated. "Well, I guess it takes time in a place like this," was the best he could manage in the way of explanation. "There's a lot of fellows who would like to come from behind and take over Palmer's position themselves."

"Humph! Tell your candidate to shake a leg, will you?" But Madge understood him fully, relieved that the ponderous wheels might already be turning.

After more hurried talk Madge allowed the young couple a few moments to themselves. Then Kip decided nervously that he must go. He slipped through the window, deep silence following his wary departure; but ten minutes went by before the unbroken stillness allowed them to hope he had made it safely.

Ezra grabbed Colerain roughly as he stole into camp, and lectured him severely. Kip took it humbly; but in the morning he marched up to Stevens, demanding to know what was being accomplished. Pat was forced to confess their meager record, although the discovery of India's whereabouts was an undeniable triumph in itself. Kip had already hurdled that point and now hungered for the next step. Spink, who had entered the conversation, was short with the puncher. They were depending on Gentry to lay the groundwork for the next move, he pointed out, and all knew as much, including Kip.

The latter burst out in exasperation. "You do nothing and don't know a thing!" he charged angrily. "Hang it, I'll haul India out of here by myself. I swear I can do it quicker! I won't leave her at the mercy of those wolves, and that's flat!"

"Easy, Colerain." Pat attempted to placate him. "A wrong move right now could ruin this whole deal. Some of us may never get out."

"Then we're mighty poor help for those women!" Kip began to argue hotly, but Pat silenced him.

"We all owe Spink something," he reminded the boy soberly. "If he hadn't got us in here we'd never have found the girl. At the Roost we're just another bunch of owlhoots. Hasn't it occurred to you what will happen if they gang up on us? You'd never get yourself back to Powder Valley, let alone India!"

Kip subsided grudgingly, but was considerably calmer after that. Paying small heed to the activities of the others, it was all he could do to wait for the return of night. Spink, who was by no means as dull as he appeared, forestalled the young puncher's attempt to steal away from camp after the evening meal.

"I know where you're goin'. Take me with yuh," he growled shortly. "I want to see Madge bad."

Though he protested at first Kip finally allowed himself to be persuaded. At the same midnight hour as before Kip slipped toward the dark hotel with Helm moving ghostlike at his heels. They were able this time to escape detection altogether, perhaps because there had been high revelry tonight in the still noisy bar.

Kip tapped at the girl's window, and after a delay it slid quietly open. He climbed through. But when Spink attempted to follow, a forbidding face appeared to confront him.

"Who is that?" There was keen suspicion in Madge's hostile demand.

"Now, ma'am—keep your voice down. Please! I just want to talk to yuh a minute—explain to yuh—"

"Explain nothing! You and your big talk! . . . Tell me I can ride out of here tomorrow with my girl, and I'll listen."

"Madge—please—" Spink groaned, peering anxiously about. It seemed to him that her strident hiss was certain to betray them. "Let me in, and we'll settle this. Your way, I promise yuh!" It was an abject plea.

"Not a bit of it," she snorted fiercely. "No excuse will get you in here now or later. Fight your own battles, Helm Spink—since mine mean nothing to you!"

Totally unable to suppress her mother's noisy defiance, India turned impulsively to Colerain. Squeezing her hand, Kip moved to the front of the place and peered guardedly out. He was back in a hurry.

"You're bein' heard," he warned the pair at the window sharply. "There's a bunch gathering in front of the bar ready for some move—"

Madge swung about angrily, instantly up in arms. "I'll fix that." Thrusting past Kip and the girl and grabbing up a stout billet of wood, she marched straight out the front door. "One side, you!" Unceremoniously scattering the grim-faced group before the bar, she strode straight into the place.

"What do you mean by this ungodly racket?" she bellowed. "At such an hour the pack of you ought to be ashamed!"

Lant Palmer was here, and he turned deliberately. "By God, this is too much! Make yourself scarce, woman!" he thundered, attempting to cow her with his deadly stare.

"Not before a lot of others! Scum like yourself!" Elbowing Palmer unceremoniously aside, Madge brandished her cedar chunk at the astounded owlhoots lined up before the bar. "Come on—clear out, the kit and boiling of you! Quick, now!"

They sought clumsily to avoid her sweeping blows but were too petrified to organize any real defense. First one, then another darted for the door. In a bare moment they were tumbling madly over one another to escape; and Madge did not stop till the barkeep himself scuttled to safety.

Warned by Sam Sloan, who came running with the news, Pat calmly watched the businesslike rout from a safe distance. He was able to intercept Spink and the puncher as they were prudently stealing back to camp before their presence at the hotel was discovered.

"You can thank Madge this time for your getaway," he remarked scathingly. "She never gave those birds much of a chance to think of anything but their own skins."

"Well—it was Spink's fault," protested Kip. "He thought he could talk her around. I was a fool to listen to him!"

"That's just like a danged woman anyhow," snarled Helm in a rage. "Give yuh away first with her big-mouthed blat—and then cover yuh while yuh run. Hanged if I know why I bother about her at all!"

Pat covertly suppressed a chuckle. Though he made no more than a shrewd guess at what had happened he was not far wrong; nor did Madge Pickett's reaction surprise him in the least. She was, he suddenly realized, enjoying all this to the hilt.

Spink, however, took the situation more seriously. "This may be a laugh for some, Stevens. It'll end in wholesale killing," he predicted gloomily, "if I don't stop Palmer's outfit cold and get those women out of here before they ruin everything!"

15.

JACK GENTRY ENJOYED what he considered an enviable reputation at Robber's Roost. One of that wily breed who look shrewdly to the future, he had taken pains to claim common cause with the various factions that made up the loose and changing confederation of the camp.

It was in his vain and egotistical nature to forward his own private interests vigorously. Even while professing to champion Helm Spink over his bitter rival, Jack was cunningly playing one man off against the other.

India Pickett was still Gentry's chief object. He had earnestly wanted the girl—in fact, thought he had her—and was secretly furious when Spink unexpectedly appeared with her mother. But Jack was no fool. Suavely masking his chagrin, he had disarmed the big outlaw with smooth diplomacy while he bided his time.

All too clearly he saw the impasse presented by Pat Stevens and his friends. A lesser man would have tried to get rid of them by crude exposure; but Gentry saw his own downfall in that poor expedient. The solution was inextricably bound up with his feelings about India, whom he honestly hoped to win over, given enough time. He dared not employ a course she would be certain to condemn. Despite all that Stevens had done for him—or perhaps perversely because of it—he hated the stalwart rancher. Shortly after his failure to reach India by means of his note (couldn't she see that *he* was, of all these men, her strongest bulwark?) Gentry turned his mind to the problem of Stevens's destruction. With Pat out of the way, Spink's menace would be negligible.

Jack sought his solution typically, by means of an elaborate lie. He had watched Lant Palmer's flat gaze travel over India on the occasion of their one meeting, and had guessed the outlaw leader's thought. It pleased him to trade now on this knowledge.

"It was Stevens's idea to bring the girl here," he told Lant carelessly one day. "Spink's in solid with her ma. Stevens persuaded him to throw India in your way. It was just another way to trip you. They figured you'd be easier to knock over—and I had to pretend to go along with that."

For a brief instant Palmer's dull eyes showed fierce life. "Like that, eh?" His jaws corded in anger.

"Sure. I figured a word to wise yuh up would be smart." Jack winked, waiting confidently for the lightning to strike. Palmer would use every lethal resource at his command if sufficiently aroused. He could have Pat Stevens quietly killed without any great exertion on his part.

"All right, Gentry. You're a pal of mine. You've said so," Palmer stated tonelessly. "Prove it this time."

Jack's brows rose in astounded protest. "Yuh mean—"

"You know what I mean." With this iron command the outlaw leader turned on his heel and slouched off.

Jack's hair prickled at the back of his skull as he stood there scowling thunderously. He was practical enough to feel strong disgust at his own ineptness. "Damn him!" he growled angrily. "I delicately hint that Stevens should be knocked off—and he hands me the job! Kind of a neat backfire, if anyone should ask." He laughed ruefully, then as swiftly sobered. "Maybe it ain't such a bad idea at that."

While he could have performed the job without reference to anyone, he did not regret that Lant Palmer knew what he was going to do. Gentry swiftly saw that he might later make shrewd use of the circumstance.

He had already surveyed Stevens's camp and knew roughly what he would have to deal with. The habits of its inmates were less familiar to him. There was only one remedy for this, and he forthwith set about climbing to a niche on the slope of a high rocky bulge above the dells. From here Gentry had a partial view of the camp. Decid-

MAN FROM ROBBER'S ROOST

ing there would be no better vantage point offered, he spent several patient hours in vigilant observation.

If there was a pattern in the quiet actions of the men he watched he was unable to figure it out. But he lay there long enough to assure himself that Stevens was often in sight in the camp below and that there would be no great difficulty in getting a fair shot at him. Jack had no rifle with him this afternoon; and it was not the only time he clambered stealthily to the spot unarmed. He was to spend the better part of two days carefully studying the movements of his quarry, being sure in the meantime to show himself now and then about the Roost. Ready to act at last, Gentry made for his niche toward graying dusk of the second day packing a high-powered rifle. He had had the forethought to borrow this latter from Lant Palmer himself.

Settling down carefully, he judged the conditions of his task. It was not too dark for a dependable sight at this distance of about two hundred yards. Yet it was shadowy enough to insure his own secure retreat once the deed was done.

What Gentry did not know was that Kip Colerain had been prowling about the crests around the Roost for purposes of his own. Kip was returning to camp late, guarding alertly against his own discovery, when wholly by accident he spotted Gentry's stealthy movements in a fold of the weather-worn rocks.

Colerain ducked and scrambled, not aware at first on whom he was spying; but when he finally recognized that hawk face in silhouette he tightened up in a flash. Kip was plunged into a quandary, since he was a distance away and armed only with his Colt. Once warned, Jack could pick him off with the rifle before he had a chance. He made sure where the renegade settled, then dropped down to begin his stealthy, creeping stalk.

Gentry, meanwhile, oblivious of all save his own fell purpose, scanned the camp below intently. Not all of the men were there, but he saw Stevens leisurely preparing supper with Sam Sloan and Spink. This was all he needed. Preparing deliberately, he rested the rifle on a smooth stone hump, setting the sights and drawing a careful bead on his unwitting victim. He was not satisfied, however, and taking his time, tried again. Pat Stevens stood still for the moment directly in his sights, and utterly without compunction Gentry slowly squeezed off his shot.

In the instant of firing he knew his luck. Too late for Gentry to check himself, Pat abruptly bent down to move something on the fire; and the leaden slug whizzed over his back with inches to spare. The bullet ricocheted off rock, and a split-second later the men at the fire had dived to cover. Inwardly raging, Gentry sprang to his feet, clapping the rifle to his shoulder again. It still might not be too late to mend things.

At that instant a harsh voice tore through Jack from directly behind. "Gentry! You crawling sidewinder—" It was Kip, beside himself with fury and not a dozen feet away. "Here's where I let you have it!"

Jack whirled wildly, his boot slipping on the slippery rock. His rifle clattered, and he went down with a shattering jar on one elbow. Gentry thrashed over on his back as Colerain, swiftly altering his plan of attack, launched himself on the other in a dive. He landed squarely on target with a thudding shock.

Stunned and desperate, Gentry tried to hurl the enraged Kip off, finding to his dismay that his one arm had gone numb and dead. Colerain meanwhile was smashing savagely at his face and banging him ruthlessly against the unyielding rock.

It was darkening swiftly, and they were no more than shadowy forms thrashing about in the gray dusk. Straddling his captive, Kip missed a wild blow, which threw him off balance. In a twinkling Gentry was free and scrambling awkwardly up. In full fitness he would have been more than a match for the lighter-framed puncher. But he had only one arm, and the difficulty of maintaining any kind of an effective guard hampered him sadly. The footing, moreover, was extremely unstable, and a fall of thirty feet threatened the first misstep. The two men closed in, belting each other fiercely.

Kip never stopped to count the odds against him; but he realized in a few seconds that Gentry was wide open, and for long minutes he was able to administer bitter punishment. Jack retaliated with wild lunges, a sudden lucky sweep of his left arm toppling Kip into an unseen crevice. When the latter staggered erect, waving his arms wildly to keep his balance, the other man was gone. Colerain paused. He heard boots scrape and plunged that way till a fall sobered him. It was nearly full dark now, and he could make out nothing. But it was a grim satisfaction that he had at least given Gentry a savage beating and made him skulk away.

Jack was in a vitriolic mood as he felt his way silently down the slick rocks. Betrayed by brute luck, which had turned against him without warning, he unconsciously shifted his bitterest hatred to Colerain. It was Kip who had turned India against him from the start, and he would have to be smashed without the slightest delay. And this time Gentry did not mean to seek anyone's advice or help.

Reaching his own camp unseen, he doggedly put himself to rights. A raw bruise on one cheek was his only observable mark, though it was an hour before feeling and use returned with excruciating tingle to his arm. Grimly he worked it supple, grinding his teeth at the bitterness of his thoughts. When he was once more his old calculating self, Gentry set out for the center of camp as if nothing had happened.

The ramshackle hotel where Madge Pickett zealously guarded the girl was the big problem for him, though he knew it was most likely the same for Colerain. Probably, he thought, the puncher had been no more successful than himself in trying to reach India; but Jack could not resist prowling about the place even at this hour, his mind scheming all the while.

He was sheltered behind a ledge, contemplating the dark rear of the building with a set face, when he suddenly stiffened. Was that a dark form he saw stealing through the shadows? Gentry waited to make sure, then began to close in silently as the other slipped toward the hotel.

He managed to hear the faint tapping of fingers on a blank window, followed by the soft murmur of low voices. Exultation seized him as he recognized Colerain, and savage satisfaction overrode his astonishment at the discovery. Here was the enemy delivered into his hands!

Assuring himself with a twinge of jealousy that Kip was

actually being permitted to crawl in the window, Gentry delayed till absolute silence returned. His crafty mind churned. He knew what he meant to do—and the beauty of it was that Colerain's demise would never be traced to him.

Jack moved quietly toward the saloon and scanned its roof anxiously. It was a one-story ell slapped against the original log structure. Light seeped from a high window or two, but this was not difficult to avoid. Loud guffaws and conversation from within covered his furtive movements as he clambered on a rock and from there crawled cautiously up to the level of the roof.

It was not overly solid, but it would hold him. Wary of betraying creaks and groans, Gentry ventured only as far as was necessary toward a displaced shake through which glinted a thin shaft of light. He crouched and applied his eye to the narrow gap, finding that he was able to survey a portion of the bar.

To his grim delight Lant Palmer was there, talking over the glasses with Rufe Cagle and Durango. Jack's keen ear identified other voices. Drawing his Colt, he nodded to himself. The stage was set.

With deadly poise he leveled his gun at the aperture and suddenly fired. An echoing roar filled the noisy bar. Cagle spun around on his rubbery legs and dropped, almost brushing Palmer.

The uproar which instantly followed was more than enough to cover Gentry's retreat as he turned to slide back down the slant roof and drop to the ground. He was in obscurity at the rear of the bar, and he ran straight away from the place, aware of muffled shouts and racing boots. Owlhoots were hurrying toward the saloon, attracted by the noisy furor. Allowing several to precede him, Jack turned to race that way, bursting forward and pushing through the door with a great show of haste and concern.

"What happened?" he demanded harshly. "I heard that shot, and I think I know where it came from—" He broke off, pretending to stare in astonishment at Cagle's prone form as the angry outlaws churned about. "My God! Is that Rufe—?"

Palmer had barely got hold of his shattered nerve, and

he fixed the speaker with a dour stare. "It was Rufe," amended Lant bluntly. "Shot in the head without a chance! What do *you* know about this affair, Jack?" His tone had turned dangerous.

Gentry's hesitation was brief. "I—saw Colerain climb through a back window into the hotel," he answered in a lowered voice. "He was visiting that girl, Lant—and he's there now! He fired that slug through a chink in the wall there, from inside the hotel. It couldn't be anything else!"

The owlhoots greeted the announcement with a roar. Palmer silenced them, gesturing fiercely. He meant to retain full control of this ugly situation. "Go on," he probed, his dead eyes glaring at Gentry. "Where was you?"

"I was outside watching." Jack pretended disgust. "Five minutes more and I'd have been in here tipping you off. But he beat me to it!"

Palmer turned his glance on the blank log wall of the hotel. There were indeed chinks at various levels, though the roar of the shot which blasted Cagle down had come with such stunning surprise that it had been impossible to determine its direction. Lant's bitter mind seized at the presence of Colerain behind the log barrier, and he waved an authoritative hand.

"Go get him, boys."

The enraged owlhoots boiled out the door with Durango in the lead. He had more than sufficient reason for wanting to lay the Circle C Bar puncher by the heels, remembering events at the abandoned line camp in the Culebras and Kip's subsequent flight. Here at the Roost, Stevens and others had effectually blocked his attempts to reach Colerain—until now.

A man ran forward to bang on the hotel door as one or two others circled to guard the rear. When there was no response Durango delayed only momentarily. His rat-eyed face was lean and cruel as he whirled. "Hell! Grab one o' them corral rails," he barked. "We ain't waitin' for no invite!"

Rough hands brought the improvised battering-ram into swift play. It crashed against the door with a hollow boom, once—and then again. The door splintered and sagged.

"Once more!"

The door burst open with a bang under the final powerful blow, and Durango started to crowd in with fully a dozen men at his heels. They were met by Madge Pickett herself, who yelled at them blasphemously. But no one paid attention to her now.

"Out of the way," Durango shouted brutally. "We want that blasted cowprod, and we're gettin' him!"

They pushed past her by sheer weight of numbers, stampeding into every corner of the place in their search. Shouts rang out, and guns were brandished. Colerain was able to avoid them only for a matter of moments. He was caught halfway out of the window and dragged back.

"Here he is! We got him!" The clamor rose to fever pitch, and for a time it was nip and tuck whether the bewildered puncher, jammed this way and that in the press of bodies, would be torn to pieces.

Durango took charge of him with stern decisiveness. "Give way there." He shouldered his men aside, hauling the luckless captive along as he crowded toward the door. "Break it up! Break it up! Palmer's waitin' for this rat!"

Madge charged them heavily in one more determined attempt to rescue Kip, but she was knocked sidewise and tripped, her head banging the rough wall with a resounding thump.

The outlaws surged back into the open. Kip felt himself thrust viciously into the saloon amid cuffs and slaps that scattered what few wits he had remaining. Palmer met him anchored solidly in the center of the bar, his feet widespread. Kip had never seen a more forbidding face.

"Well, kid." Lant's rumble was deadly. "We'll give yuh a drumhead trial—but from here it looks like curtains for drillin' my friend Cagle through that wall. Yuh shouldn't have done that!"

16.

"I NEVER!"

In his confused state, Colerain was not certain what he was being accused of, though the motionless body of the slain outlaw on the floor behind Palmer offered a strong hint. From the hotel Kip had heard the muffled shot; but he was wholly ignorant of what had happened exactly or of Gentry's cold-blooded plot against him. He knew only that he was charged with the consequences of some act not his own.

Lant shook his head dourly while the stone-faced outlaws waited in deathly silence. "Too bad. Afraid yuh can't talk your way out of this one," he sneered sarcastically.

Kip saw their murderous mood, a cold sweat starting out on his brow. "I won't try, because I was never in it!" he flashed desperately.

"Come, come, boy," Palmer admonished inexorably. Not by so much as the flick of an eyelash did he acknowledge his awareness of Pat Stevens, Ezra and Spink coolly pushing into the bar, their eyes keen and watchful. Lant waved a brusque hand toward Gentry. "Didn't yuh tell me he fired that shot, Jack?"

"Sure he did—right through a chink in that wall," swore Gentry smoothly. He had never been more self-possessed. "Why, it had to be him! He was found there, wasn't he? Who else would want to down Cagle or any of us?"

"You lie, Gentry! You're doing this on account of that girl," Kip shouted.

Jack's glare was venomous. He made a contemptuous

gesture. "Turn him loose," he demanded indignantly. "I'll settle this now!"

"No yuh don't." Durango stepped in front of Colerain, his eyes dangerous. "He's ours now, Gentry! Rufe was a pal of mine. I ain't bein' cheated out of this!"

It was at this moment, in the midst of chilling silence, that Helm Spink showed his true fiber. His spur chains clinked as he strode calmly out, thrusting Durango aside with a massive hand, to stand shoulder-to-shoulder beside Kip.

"What are yuh aimin' to do with this boy, Lant?" he rumbled flatly.

Palmer's weatherbeaten face was inscrutable. "We'll hang him, Spink," he said in a startlingly soft tone.

"What for?"

Palmer waved a careless hand behind him. "For sinkin' a slug in Cagle here. It's been proved on him—if that means anything to yuh."

"It don't," Helm spat. "Especially comin' from you *or* Gentry." His harsh breathing could be heard plainly. "I wouldn't believe it now if I saw it myself!"

Palmer realized fully just what he was up against here. Neither Spink nor Stevens worried him too much in the presence of a score or more of his own crowd. But he was not prepared to force an issue in which he would plainly be expected to take the lead. It might still be possible to accomplish their defeat by craft.

"You brought this kid into the Roost, didn't you?" asked Lant pointedly. "I heard you had a difference about it with Cagle on the trail—"

"If I shot Rufe Cagle I'd do it under your nose!" roared Helm angrily. "I don't depend on somebody else, like I hear is popular here! . . . Kip never did that job, Palmer, and be damned to yuh!"

"Sho," Palmer's scorn was faint. "You wouldn't be favorin' a —recent friend now, Spink?"

"Anytime, Palmer," retorted the big man grimly. "Where you're concerned!"

The two natural enemies measured each other bleakly. If an effort had been made to gloss over the antagonism between them it was useless now. Fire flew from their crossed glances, and the outlaw leader's leathery face slowly grew mottled.

"Throwin' your double cross right in my teeth, are yuh?" he ground out, realizing with chill certainty that he was being shoved toward a showdown by this man who had always questioned his dominance. The tough outlaw pack stood about in breathless quiet like wolves, ready to spring on the loser.

"Have it your way, Lant. You wouldn't have it no different!"

Palmer stiffened. A deep, bitter dread of Helm Spink had always plagued him, motivating his extravagant attempts to ensure that Spink never came back to the Roost. Everything had failed, and here was the sorry result. Lant knew, as he had long guessed, that there was to be no evading this moment.

Watching narrowly, Stevens caught the swift gathering of the outlaw's forces. Palmer's dead pupils sharpened to piercing pinpoints; his slack shoulders tensed. In the yellow light of the hanging coal oil lamp his draw was a flashing blur of movement. Spink rolled his Colt up simultaneously with the apparent clumsiness and lightning swiftness of a grizzly's striking paw.

Gunfire blasted thunderously. In the blue billow of smoke that rose between the two figures Helm Spink stood rocklike. It was Palmer who faltered, the burning hatred fading from his contorted face. Lant slowly collapsed, turning sidewise, his support melting from under him. He slumped to the plank floor with a rattling thump half across Rufe Cagle's legs, and his gun bounced noisily against the bar.

"You downed him! By gravy, Spink, that's too much!" Durango yelled fiercely at the big man, his rat-eyes aflame with fury. "Are we standin' for this, boys?"

He was making his vengeful appeal directly to the outlaws, and it was not hard to guess his motive. As Palmer's confederate and a crony of Gentry's, he had worked against the man who had promised in a single stroke to usurp the fallen leader's power. Durango understood that he could expect short shrift at Spink's hands. With Helm torn down in retaliation, however, Durango not only had a chance but he himself might even become head of the pack.

Pat also was swift to follow implications to their logical end, though he went far beyond Durango in evaluating the moment's meaning for them all. Stevens held no brief for Spink as an outlaw playing his own dangerous game; but with Helm gone India Pickett would stand no chance of getting out of this mess unscathed, nor would any of them be in a much better situation.

Spink meanwhile was of no mind to let matters get out of hand if he could help it. "Hold it, Durango! Right where yuh are," he droned. "It ain't a question of what you'll stand for! I'm the boss here, if you're slow on the uptake." His bright stare was challenging. "Lant had to be persuaded the hard way. If you're honin' to be next, mister, fly at it!"

Jack Gentry, who had been following events closely if unobtrusively, saw quickly enough in which direction Spink's mind was moving. If Helm could keep the opposition to his leadership on a man-to-man level his final triumph was assured. Gentry courted further involvement to the extent of trying to block this shrewd game.

"Don't fall for that, Durango," he flashed. "This concerns the whole Roost. Let the boys themselves decide what they'll do about it!"

This was the split-second break Pat Stevens had been waiting for. He pushed coolly through the crowd of outlaws and gave Jack a stiff-arm thrust that sent him lurching out on the open floor as the center of attraction. Without pause Pat followed close to give the wily renegade a fixed and deadly stare.

"Now we'll come down to cases, Gentry," he rapped. "I was waiting for you to speak out of turn."

Gentry glared back in surprised and hostile resentment. "What are you driving at, Stevens?"

"You know what I am getting at! It was you who set off this whole affair. It wasn't Colerain who shot Cagle in the first place, and you know it. Because you did it yourself!"

Jack staged a dramatic show of furious indignation. "What kind of hogwash is this?" he flamed. "I don't think these boys want to listen to—"

"Let them decide, mister! It's your idea," Pat's voice

MAN FROM ROBBER'S ROOST 133

rang out. "You were mighty quick to pin the job on Kip. It was a convenient way to cover up yourself!"

"Pah! Talk," sneered Gentry. "Your word won't clear Colerain any quicker than it'll convict me. Such as it is, you're wearing your welcome plenty thin, Stevens!"

"Then we'll have a few facts." Pat grew stern. "You might notice that Colerain isn't packing a gun in his holster. He wasn't when he was dragged out of that hotel—because Mrs. Pickett wouldn't let him wear one in her home. Kip *couldn't* have shot Cagle unless he used a peashooter!"

Gentry began to laugh sardonically, aware of how he must impress the outlaws. "That's a likely yarn," he scoffed.

"All right, find the gun," invited Pat tersely. "There isn't one in that whole place! It's a cinch you never supplied the girl with one when you dragged her here. If Madge Pickett was carrying one when she drove you out, she never bothered to use it!" He paid no heed to the grim chuckles evoked by his satire. "Call the woman in here. She'll settle the question of whether a shot was fired from that hotel if there is an argument!"

Jack was plainly not anxious to have this point pursued. "I expect we can trust that old bat to hide a gun so it'll never be found . . . You still don't make sense out of a weak attempt to accuse me, and I don't like it!"

Jack's friends in the place began to mutter angrily and to toss black looks in Stevens's direction. Then a voice broke in on them dryly from the other side of the crowded room.

"Nobody expects yuh to like it, Gentry. But don't do nothin' hasty, all the same!"

Sam Sloan had been the last to make an unobtrusive entrance, and he had edged his way to a position separated from the others that gave a clear view of the disputants. Gun in hand, he crouched alertly against the log wall effectively covering Pat; and Jack belatedly noticed Ezra was also covering from the other side. Stevens ignored the interruption, his attention never leaving the scowling renegade.

"Then I'll make it plainer." Pat's level look pinned

Gentry where he stood. "The slug that killed Cagle never came through those logs at all. Take a look at what it did to his jaw." He pointed accusingly at the dead outlaw. "Any fool could tell that bullet was traveling downward! It took Cagle in the side of the face and came out under his chin. It couldn't have done that coming from any one of those chinks!"

Jack went pasty. "What do you draw from that?" came his husky words.

"Why, that you climbed up and fired through the shakes of this roof," Pat retorted coldly. "You counted on the surprise and the racket to befuddle these men about just where the shot came from. Your scheme almost worked, Gentry!"

Jack heard him out with dismay. He found it impossible to credit his having been seen. He had been too careful. Pat must have made a wild guess that hit the truth by a mere fluke of chance—it could be no more.

"You're a cute one, Stevens!" Jack bolstered his tottering position by pretending sarcastic admiration. "You know how to twist words. There still ain't a thing but your say-so to show I had anything whatever to do with this!"

"No?" Pat whipped out a hand to whirl the renegade around to the light, at the same time sweeping his palm downward across Gentry's shirt front. A tiny shower of woody fragments pattered to the floor. "What are these shake splinters doing on your clothes? There's not another roof in the whole Roost that you could have picked them up from."

This was a graphic and striking demonstration of Gentry's guilt. Not one of the closely watching owlhoots questioned its conclusive logic. Yet there were those who found good reason to meet the renegade's merciless exposure with some chagrin.

A clamor of arguments and hot recriminations arose, causing momentary confusion. In the midst of it Kip Colerain sprang toward Gentry, his face furious.

"*You're* responsible for the killing you tried to pin on me, you dog!"

Though he was unarmed he smashed a blow to Jack's jaw, attempting at the same time to hurl the man to the floor. Stevens and Spink thrust forward quickly, intent on preventing a wild melee that might have an unfavorable outcome. But they were too late—the outlaws had closed in on the struggling antagonists.

Buffeted and half-stunned, Kip felt his grip torn from the renegade. It was all he could do to keep from winding up on the floor under the mob's stamping boots. Gentry's cronies, shrewdly led by Durango, swept Jack back, effectively separating him from his foes. He was still not out of the bar; but the object of his reckless and determined supporters was plain.

Trap Hagen sought to block the play, charging Durango savagely. "I been wantin' a crack at you, Durango!" he blazed. "Finishin' off Fred Sparks comes high in my book, and here's where you pay up!"

"Flip your ace, Hagen!" Durango was fully as ready for war. "I don't object to sendin' yuh after him!"

The owlhoots reacted furiously to this exploding feud, and they jammed in a mass around the fiercely contesting pair. Pat apprehensively watched the fight for the glint of a drawn gun, since at this point flying lead could wreak terrible havoc.

No guns appeared; but Gentry and his friends took prompt advantage of this effective confusion. Closing ranks, they broke for the door. Spink tried to break up the move, only to be hurtled aside. In less than a matter of seconds Gentry stood triumphantly in the dark entrance, flashing a look back over his shoulder. Then he faded into the gloom beyond.

"Don't let him get away!" Kip cried out in fierce alarm. But no one had any intention of allowing the slippery renegade to escape. Pat, Spink and the others forced their way toward the open, accompanied less quickly by some neutral outlaws who were inclined to blame Gentry.

"Keep him away from the horses!" Sam Sloan sang out as they raced into the clearing about the hotel. Though there was the sound of stamping boots no sign appeared of fleeing forms in the thickness of the night. But everyone knew where the men would be certain to head.

Some distance from the hotel a general corral had been thrown up in a space free of the granite ridges and dykes that made up the dells. There were always a score or more of broncs behind the sagging poles of the big pen.

They ran that way, guns out. Suddenly Ezra fired, the orange flame of his shot lancing the shadows. A man yelled, and there instantly followed the clatter of a dropped corral pole as whoever sought to snake out mounts beat a further hasty retreat.

"Gentry wasn't in that bunch!" exclaimed Trap Hagen. "He made off some other way. It'd be like him to circle back and crawl into the hotel to hide!"

This made sense. Moreover, Pat knew Jack used a secluded camp removed from the center of activities, and it followed that he would keep his horse isolated as well.

"Spread out and rake this camp to the bottom," ordered Pat swiftly. "Don't leave so much as a rock unturned—and shoot the instant you see his face!"

Separating, they worked quickly and thoroughly through the Roost. It was Pat himself who knocked at the hotel door and conferred hurriedly with the ruffled and by now badly worried Madge. She had seen nothing of Gentry. The others soon returned, gloomy of expression. Not only had Durango and his confederates seemingly faded into thin air, but it was increasingly plain that Gentry himself had given them the slip and made his escape.

Ezra was the last to appear. With his usual skill he had located the renegade's hidden camp. His report was brief. Not only was the man himself gone but his horse as well. The evidence was conclusive. Gentry was unquestionably well on his way toward distant parts.

17.

HELM SPINK WAS ENRAGED. He tramped back and forth in the clearing before the hotel, snarling at the owlhoots who stood about. "You know now who the double-crosser was around here," he blazed significantly. His broad-shouldered frame and flashing eyes dominated them all.

"Gentry broke his neck to queer me and my friends! It wasn't three hours ago he tried to bushwhack us in our camp! Colerain caught him at it and almost killed him. So what does Jack do but blast Rufe Cagle from cover and lay it to the boy! There's Lant Palmer's pal for you, and I hope you like him!"

Though in one respect a needless waste of time, the huge outlaw's rant was not without deep design. His listeners growled angrily at Gentry's scheming duplicity which had already been responsible for several deaths.

"What'll yuh do, Spink? Is that hydrophoby skunk gettin' away with this?"

A variety of questions were tossed at Helm. It was plain these men were waiting for his decision, and this was all he needed. Reinstated by a series of rapid events no one could have foreseen, Helm took charge with cold precision.

"Get up the horses," he barked at Sam Sloan. "We ain't waiting for daylight. There's a lot of ways out of this place, but Gentry's bound to stick to one trail or the other. We'll overhaul him tomorrow, and I aim to have a talk with that hombre!"

With Gentry and Durango in full flight and their supporters scattered, no further restraint hampered Spink and the others. Colerain was in a tearing hurry to get started, and he ran with Sam and Ezra to saddle the broncs.

A dozen or more resentful owlhoots put in an appearance before the hotel, mounted and ready to join in the pursuit. Helm had ideas of his own, but he was too shrewd to precipitate an argument. In clipped accents he named off groups, assigning each its task.

"Bandy, you and your boys take the trail to Brown's Park," he instructed a squat, bowlegged man. "You should pick up Gentry's sign by daylight if he went that way— and mind, I want that wolf dragged back here, feet first or any way you have to do it!"

A second group was dispatched on the rugged trail that led south through the badlands to one or two isolated Mormon villages on the wild Utah border. Their orders were the same. Once found, Gentry was to be brought back to the Roost to answer for his crimes. Finally, only Spink and the men who had accompanied him from Powder Valley were left. The giant slowly swung astride and turned to face them.

"All primed, are yuh? It's up to us to cover the Green River trail," he barked. "If Jack was unlucky enough to run that way he's our bacon!"

They set off without further ado, Pat and Spink in the lead. There was no useless display of haste however. The rugged character of the ground forbade it, and all knew that if Gentry was to avoid accident his pace could be little better than their own. The renegade would depend on steady travel during the dark hours to put distance between himself and any possible pursuit.

"I hope you're figuring to string that bird up right where we nail him," Colerain remarked, crowding up beside Helm. "He don't deserve anything better, and you can bet he knows it!"

Pat waited for the reply. He had wisely refrained from protesting Spink's folly at the time the oily-tongued Gentry had talked him into a plot against Palmer. Helm had been blinded then by an intense desire to drag down his rival at any cost, but his eyes were open now.

"He'll sure be watchin' for us, boy—if he lasts long enough to get a rope around his neck," Spink rumbled.

MAN FROM ROBBER'S ROOST 139

"There ain't a one of us he didn't make a fool of, and I'm the biggest of all! Can't figure out now why it took me so long to see through him!"

Pat could have told him that Madge Pickett's common sense and resentment had much to do with his final awakening. But perhaps this would dawn on the man with passing time. "How sure can we be of which way that rat will run?" he queried, changing the subject abruptly.

Helm shook his head knowingly. He turned cold and businesslike. "He'll head east. Gentry's washed up in owlhoot country. No man with backbone will put up with him a minute after the deal he handed Cagle. He knows that much."

Ezra was inclined to agree. "He'll get out from under in a hurry, providin' he can make it," he seconded. His terse tone said that the renegade would not have much luck if he could prevent it.

"Hurry it up, can't you?" Kip, already well in the lead, called back impatiently. They heard the hoofs of his bronc scrape perilously on the bare rock, proving there was no safe travel down the miles of winding trail from Robber's Roost to Green River.

"Snaffle that itch of yours, boy," Sam called after him gruffly. "We all feel the same as you do. Pushin' the ponies now is just playin' Gentry's game."

The moon, growing later with passing days, at last loomed up over the canyon wall to afford them partial aid. The weather had turned cold at dark, and the night was raw and blustery. Even now scudding clouds obscured the moonlight, and Pat studied their dun outlines with growing concern. Sam observed his preoccupation.

"Don't like the looks of that sky a bit, do yuh," he charged.

Pat's headshake was bothered. "It smells like a storm, Sam. I hope I'm wrong; but winter can't be far off," he ventured uneasily. "When it comes it'll close up this high country tighter than a drum. I expect those hombres at the Roost pile into the hotel and let it howl—but we can't afford to get snowed in back here in the wilds until spring!"

All of them knew the season had been getting on, for the white patches grew on the tallest peaks, and the ice in the creeks took longer to melt each day. They had closed their eyes to these warnings, hoping for a break. Up until the present, certainly, it had been impossible to withdraw from the mountains, taking the women with them. Pat wondered whether they should not have brought Madge and India along tonight and made an effort—regardless of the outcome of this chase—to strike on through to lower country before it was too late.

Gradually the clouds thickened and a cutting wind whistled through the gloomy canyon. It grew pitch dark, showing their advance to a blundering walk. They knew what they were up against when freezing pinpricks of moisture began to drive into their numb faces.

"Snow!" Kip exclaimed. "That's all we need to stop us cold—"

They drove on, doggedly silent, their collars turned up against the raw blast and hands thrust into their pockets. One or two donned slickers. The storm blew fitfully, a white pall descending to swirl about them for minutes, leaving them in utter confusion, then slacking off. Gradually the rocks were plastered with a clinging snow which gave them a ghostly gray pallor.

Dawn came on at last, dim, bleak, and bitterly cold. They clung stubbornly to the trail, though it was half an hour before they could see objects close at hand with any clearness. A thin skiff of snow lay over the trail, hiding it effectually.

"Look at that!" Colerain remarked bitterly. "Not a chance of tracking even an elephant under that cover! Unless we come up on Gentry, we're licked. And he's a good hour ahead of us at least!"

"Don't be so sure." Ezra spoke gruffly from behind his upturned collar. He waved a hand toward the gray sky, which showed signs of breaking. "Gentry's bound to leave tracks in this stuff, and it'll never warm up enough today to melt off. It could be he's the one who made a big mistake!"

Travel was brisker now that the snow had stopped. They were descending deeper into the gaping canyons with every mile; the ragged, bastioned walls rose hundreds of feet above their heads, closing in the sullen sky. If Gentry had indeed come this way there was no chance for him to deviate from the straight trail. He could only drive ahead, hoping to keep his lead.

Suddenly Kip gave a triumphant yell and pointed downward into the snow. Peering, Ezra saw the faint outline of a hoofprint. He nodded.

"The snow was already slackin' off when he made that," he growled. "Them tracks'll be plainer from now on."

This proved to be the case, and unconsciously they thrust on at an increased pace until they were within easy striking distance of Green River ford. On this side of the river the rocky walls were eroded and chopped up into a broken snarl. If Jack could break his trail he might yet succeed in eluding them by hiding in some craggy recess while they passed unawares within a matter of yards.

They alerted, studying the gaps and ledges and scanning the twisting gullies. All knew Gentry's horse, a bright chestnut. Its distinctive, elongated hoofprint was not easily mistaken. Ezra had taken a grim satisfaction in pointing out that without doubt this was the horse ahead of them now.

They had begun to follow an open stretch of the canyon where the telltale tracks led on before them straight and clear. Suddenly a leaden slug tore a corner off the crumbling red ledge over their heads, showering Pat and Spink with sandstone splinters. The heavy gunshot echoed weirdly through the crags and crannies of the lonely amphitheater.

"Watch it!" Sam cried. "He's up there in the rocks somewheres, and he's packin' a carbine!"

They scattered hastily, seeking the cover of ledge and boulder. Yanking their own rifles from the saddle boots, they warily studied the broken maze of rocks surrounding them. It was no simple matter they were up against. If Gentry had holed up to waylay them from cover, he must have selected some well-protected niche from which the approaches could be easily guarded. It would not be easy to locate, for the wind that howled through the rocks ruined any effective sense of direction.

Aware of this they clung closely to cover, and slow

moments passed without any further development. Sam finally boldly risked disaster by pushing into the open in dogged pursuit of the enemy's betraying tracks. Immediately the hidden carbine crashed again, and Sam's hat tore off his head. He dived from the saddle to snatch it up, dragging his bronc back to shelter.

"Good work, Sam! But don't try that crazy stunt again," Pat called across warningly.

Sloan ground-anchored his pony and, clinging to the cover of a gully, crawled on hands and knees to where Pat, Ezra and Spink were coolly conferring. "Did yuh spot him?" he asked, grinning unabashed.

Pat's nod was curt. "The shot came from somewhere up on that tangle of ridges." He waved toward where the lofty canyon wall had broken down into a series of seamed and crumbling humps. "How in time Gentry ever managed to get a bronc up there I'll never know."

"Maybe he didn't," suggested Ezra. "If he cached it somewhere and crawled up there, we can cut him off. Corner him where he is and it's all over!"

"That's easy said." Pat's grunt was practical. "We'll spread out and try to close in. Tell Colerain what to do as you crawl back that way, Sam—and I needn't warn any of you what we're up against!"

Without further words they set grimly about the task of trapping the treacherous marksman, spreading out along the broken ridge and working laboriously upward. It meant creeping across the freezing, snow-covered rock at considerable cost to raw fingers, and their bodies soon grew numb and stiff. Colerain, in his driving impatience, was prone to press on dangerously in advance of the others. More than once Stevens, from a protected spot, was forced to wave the young fellow back. All Kip would consent to do was wait till they caught up with him. Then he forged on, plainly driven by an overwhelming urge to come to grips with his foe.

Shortly after their start the quarry unleashed a barrage of racketing shots, advertising his awareness of their purpose. After that a dead silence descended, broken only by the drone of the bitter wind. Colerain worked steadily toward the top of the ridge, taking fearful chances in the determined effort to locate Gentry's position. Not even Pat's sharp call could hold him back now.

Suddenly Kip leaped to his feet and dashed for the rugged crest, the echoes clattering as he blasted a string of shots down the far slope of the ridge. "Get back to the broncs," he bawled, whirling as the others thrust their heads above the rocks in astonishment and alarm. "Our bird's flushed! I saw him down there scrambling aboard his bronc. Give him ten minutes and he'll be gone!"

They hastily turned back down the rough slope, leaping and sliding. It was only a matter of minutes before they piled aboard their mounts and raced for the lower end of the ridge. With farther to climb down, Kip was behind the others, though he came racing after at a breakneck pace.

They came too late upon a fresh trail gouged deeply into the snow. The quarry had given them the slip once more, but at least they had him on the run. They shoved after, determined that this time the chase would not be long.

It was Pat who presently threw up a hand and pointed far ahead. "There he goes!" He had caught a flash of flickering red down the canyon. "That's Gentry's horse, and no mistake about it!"

Near its junction with the awe-inspiring charm of the Green, the canyon split into a series of incredibly rough branches. A number of rocky mouths opened away from the main gorge, many of them hidden by high shoulders or jumbled heaps of broken rock. It was possible for the fugitive to turn into any of these in his attempt to throw them off. They had lost sight of him almost at once beyond the intervening boulders; and here the screaming gusts of wind had swept the revealing snow from the rocks, banking it in crevices or whirling it into the air in blinding clouds.

Ezra hauled up sharply at the mouth of a gulch when the others would have driven past. "This way, Stevens!" He pointed down at the slick rock underfoot. They drove through the gulch and started to climb.

"There he goes! We're cutting his lead down fast!"

Looking where Kip pointed they saw the straining rider far ahead, hurling his horse up the steep ascent. He struck sliding shale, but after a tense moment of fighting his mount he forged steadily on. The white patch of his face was turned backward, and he fired a wild shot. But the crumbling red spires and weathered ledges interfered with his aim. On they toiled, unable to gain materially but never losing sight of their quarry.

It was a punishing climb. They came out at last on a cracked, lofty rim and circled around to the right. Here the wind screamed unimpeded off ice-clad peaks, and it penetrated to the marrow.

"Look! Look!" Sam pointed directly across the circular chasm yawning under the rim. The man they pursued was working doggedly along a wide ledge on the opposite rim. If he could reach its end and climb a hundred-yard slant he might yet escape over a swell that led on to distant canyons.

"Have t' stop that."

Ezra deliberately dismounted, rifle in hand. Resting on a rock and unhurriedly gauging the wind, he fired. They could make out no immediate effect beyond a slight increase in the quarry's pace. Ezra again calmly took aim, delaying this time until it seemed he would never pull the trigger.

Crack! The explosion was whipped away with the wind. Colerain gave a strangled cry.

"You got him! . . . My God, what a shot, Ezra!"

The escaping man had slipped down from the saddle to lie huddled on the exposed rock. They had no inkling of how badly he was hit, but he did not move. It took them half an hour to follow the rim around; nearing the still form, Kip slid down from his bronc to run forward. They saw him stiffen as he had his careful look. Then he turned, his face strained and white.

"This isn't Gentry at all!" he burst out in hoarse dismay. "It's Durango! They switched horses, damn their slippery souls! Durango took Jack's bay and led us all over hell's half acre on a fool's chase!" His tense voice cracked as he concluded tragically. "By this time Gentry's probably miles away and laughing up his sleeve at us!"

18.

THE SOBERING DISCOVERY that Jack Gentry was not the man they pursued gave rise to hot discussion. Durango had been shot through the chest and he had died almost at once. Gentry's horse, standing a few yards beyond with reins trailing, was mute evidence of his trickery.

Since they had followed only one set of tracks there was good reason to believe that Jack had never ridden this way at all.

"Trap Hagen named it," Kip spoke up uneasily as the reality of their situation sank home. "He said it would be like Gentry to hide right there in the Roost! If that's what he did, you know what India and her mother have been up against!"

The thought drew their faces taut. Pat was the first to regain his balance. "Hold on now," he said levelly. "Gentry pulled a neat one on us by switching horses with Durango—that's true. But I don't believe he's fool enough to stay very long at the Roost. He hasn't a single friend there; and he knows we'll be back."

"It would still give him plenty of time to grab that girl and run," pointed out Sam shrewdly. "With the lot of us hightailin' off like this to leave him a clear field—"

"Well, he's still got Madge to get around," Spink said practically. "Cheer up, Kip. She sent Gentry packin' once. If I know her, she can do it again just as quick!"

They all knew, however, that even Madge Pickett's doughty opposition would be useless before Gentry's guns. Jack would not boggle at her murder to gain his ends.

"All the same, we've got to get back there fast!"

Colerain agitated. "I'll never rest till I know that wolf is safe under the sod!"

It was obvious how he felt, and the others, moreover, were well equipped to sympathize with him; but Pat quickly prevented the puncher from turning his bronc on the spot and starting back for the Roost.

"Go a little easy, boy," he cautioned. "We'll want to take Gentry's bay back with us as proof of his caper. And for another thing, we'll simply have to get out of this wind in short order and build us a fire."

Kip knew he was right. During the long ride around the exposed rim the freezing blast had ripped steadily at them. No man could stand much more of it without collapsing, and the horses were in little better shape. With typical foresight Ezra had stowed a sack of coffee in his saddlebag and wrapped a blackened pot in his slicker. Finding a sheltered corner, they built a blaze of dead cedar and stood about, slapping their arms and gratefully sipping the smoking drink.

Time had fled while they pursued the owlhoot, and it was past midmorning of a gloomy, gray and bitter day. The ride back would consume the shortening hours before early dark closed in once more.

"No help for it." Ez shook the grounds from the coffeepot and fastened it on his cantle. "Got to get goin'. We're plumb lucky that snow didn't amount to no more than it did."

"Right—and we may not have seen the last of it, either."

Pat's grave expression sent them climbing briskly into the saddle. They started on their way without further loss of time, Sam leading Gentry's horse after him.

The solitude of this barren land seemed to have increased tenfold without the incentive of a hot pursuit to drive them on, and they could not help but speculate grimly about what they might find on arrival at the Roost. Once more Colerain pushed impatiently to the fore, urging them to greater speed until he was admonished by Pat.

"Crowd that pony of yours much more without a rest and a good feed, and it'll fold."

This was so, and Kip knew it. But worry continued to plague him. "An hour or so may make all the difference for India," he jerked out unsteadily. "Spink never did any of us a favor by bringing that damned Gentry to Powder Valley! I sure wish I'd never laid eyes on either of them!"

Helm's response was surprisingly mild. "I'm tryin' to make it up to you, boy," he protested heavily. "You ain't the only one that's on my neck about it by a long shot!"

Midday passed while they climbed the canyon, and afternoon came. There was some sunlight on the rocky heights, but it was powerless to warm the freezing air, and it did not last long. The gray clouds thickened once more and the light failed quickly. Dusk was already closing in by the time they neared the Roost again.

Fires twinkled brighter than usual tonight in the dells. They could hardly wait for a glimpse of the hotel. There were signs of life there, and light gleamed from the bar. Kip raced down into the clearing, jumped from his pony and ran straight for the hotel.

He burst in at the door, a pang striking through him at the ominous fact that it was no longer barred, when a rough hand stopped him in his tracks and whirled him violently around.

"Hold on here, bucko. What do you mean by bustin' in here like that?" It was Madge's booming voice. She checked herself, peering into his face. "Why—it's Kip! Why didn't you say so right off? . . . Back again, are you." Seeming almost to forget him, she peered past the door with a trace of nervous constraint in her manner. "But where's the—rest of your crowd?"

"Right behind me." Colerain brushed this aside with an impatient gesture. "Is India all right, Mrs. Pickett?—Did you see anything more of Gentry?"

"Indy? Of course she's all right! *I'm* right here, ain't I?" Madge looked at him again searchingly. "Why are you asking all this, boy? Didn't you catch that scoundrel?"

Kip's response was interrupted by India's appearance. She was obviously excited and greeted the puncher warmly. He stared at her, scarcely able to believe in his good fortune. "What a relief," he breathed devoutly. "We overhauled Gentry's horse— and found Durango riding it! I didn't dare guess what to expect when we got back—"

"If Jack was here, we saw nothing of him," returned

the girl. They drew aside to talk, oblivious for the moment of what was going on about them.

Madge was irritable at being ignored. She stepped out importantly as the rest of Kip's party drew up before the place. "All here, I take it?" She scanned them critically. "Took you long enough, I must say . . . Well! Don't just sit there. Clean yourselves up and get in here for supper." It was a brisk and conclusive order.

They were dismounting stiffly, concluding from her competent manner that everything was under control, when Madge unexpectedly gave a harsh call. A man hurried out of the bar and came toward them. It was Galey, the cross-eyed owlhoot, and he eyed Madge with uncommon respect.

"Take care of them horses, Galey, if you've nothing better to do," she barked shortly. "Helm's plumb wore out, I judge; and so are the rest of these boys."

Galey complied with alacrity, gathering the proffered reins and leading the ponies away. Spink looked expressively at Pat and rolled his eyes as Madge turned her back to reenter the hotel.

"I'm too late, Stevens," the big outlaw muttered in a carefully guarded tone. "She's took charge here, and the rest of us will never stand a chance!"

Pat chuckled. "Which was your biggest mistake, taking Gentry to Powder Valley or bringing Madge Pickett here?" he returned dryly. Spink frowned, not appreciating the well-deserved satire.

They tramped in to find a hearty meal of venison waiting on the table. Again Helm and Colerain discovered India waiting on them, this time without Gentry to create a dissident note. Spink found time only to observe with puzzlement that Madge appeared to have softened toward him, despite her caustic comments on their failure to overtake Jack.

"Gentry's too smart for you all," she announced plainly. "I kept this place from fallin' apart while you were gone; you better run it better than you do some things!"

Whether or not her boast was literally true she had certainly assumed a fresh lease of authority during their brief absence. Pat guessed shrewdly from her management of Galey that she had the Roost squarely under her thumb and that she did not intend to relinquish her power readily. It remained to be seen whether Spink was destined for the same unceremonious treatment.

Even Sam and Ezra seemed strangely subdued tonight, content to listen while they ate. But they were firm in their determination to retire immediately afterward to their camp, and Pat joined them, confident that Colerain and Spink, whom the woman insisted should remain in the hotel, were a sufficient guard.

"Nobody's gettin' me to stay around her longer'n I have to," Ezra growled later over their fire. "She can feed me; she can't ruin my life. Spink'll wish *he'd* come away before he gets done with her, too!"

For all this, recent events at the Roost had made life easier to bear. The crusty partners could not deny a certain relief at their freedom of movement the following day. They were able to come and go at will, and Sloan took the opportunity to get acquainted with a number of easygoing owlhoots. He spent time in the bar familiarizing himself with affairs at large.

The outlaws who had taken other trails in pursuit of Gentry returned that day with little or nothing to report. They had pushed far and hard without finding any evidence whatever of the renegade's whereabouts. Jack had disappeared completely, and they proceeded to forget about him.

"One thing is certain," Sam concluded when they talked it over in private. "Gentry will never come back here. He knows what's waiting for him the minute he shows his face."

Meanwhile they saw little enough of Spink. Not even Madge was able to monopolize his time. Stating only that it was necessary, Helm took decisive charge of the Roost, conferring with one hard-faced group or another and strutting happily about in his newfound authority. He was in his natural element here, or so it seemed; and though approaching winter called a halt to the nefarious activities of the various bands, there was little doubt that he intended to assume full command of them all.

Pat put in an appearance at meals in the hotel, as Madge

urgently proposed, if only to keep close track of developments. It was disturbing to find an air of easy compliance in the masterful woman's attitude toward Spink. She appeared by no means averse to sharing his authority over the sprawling camp. Probably she would be in no hurry to bring it to an end.

Sam put a finger on the crux of the matter that night in camp. "I don't like it," he declared. "What are we waitin' for, Stevens? No good reason why we can't pull out of here now. This is just givin' Gentry time to organize a reception committee when we do leave. Spink ought t' know that much!"

Ezra spat in the fire contemptuously. "Don't expect no flash of sense out of him now. The fool's in love."

Pat nodded thoughtfully. The lanky tracker's diagnosis seemed startlingly true. Helm was undeniably in the saddle here, ostentatiously impressing his woman with his own importance. Even Madge's grim determination to get her daughter India to a place of safety appeared to waver fatally. Such a situation could lead to disaster if prolonged.

Kip himself was fully aware of this. "Put the spurs to Spink, Stevens," he urged strongly the following morning on a visit to their camp. "There's nothing to hold us here any longer. If winter clamps down we'll find ourselves in the soup!"

It was true the weather had cleared and turned mild. But such periods were deceptive at this late season, and Kip's concern was no more genuine or pressing than Pat's own.

The puncher found further cause for anxiety before the day was much older. Pat was walking toward the hotel at noon when he saw Spink rush into the adjacent saloon where an uproar of some sort was in progress. Helm soon put an end to it by booting a sullen outlaw out of the place and hauling Colerain roughly after him.

"Any more fightin'," the big man growled hardily, "and I'll sure take you in hand, boy!"

Kip tore loose with a defiant exclamation and stumped into the hotel. When Pat joined him and the others at the table a moment later he noticed that India had turned her back on the young fellow, discouragement in her face. Madge was no more solicitous, and she eyed Kip coldly.

"You're growing just as tough as the rest of these roughnecks," India charged. "I thought that was surely the last thing I needed to expect from you!"

"I'm not!" Kip denied loudly. "You know what this crowd is. But they're not walkin' over me!" he insisted, his face red.

"Why should anyone walk over you?" Madge snorted. But she was curious and plied Kip with searching questions, little as he wanted to talk. She bedeviled him unmercifully, however, beating down his evasions till he lost his temper.

"Hang it all! I slugged that mouthy bird in the bar for making a snide remark about India, if you have to know," he blurted out furiously.

Helm gave a bristling response to this challenge, his face thunderous. "Why didn't yuh tell me that?" he blared. "I'd have ruined the rat—"

Madge put an end to his rumbling bluster with cool decision. "Well, that's enough! Remarks about India indeed! I've been waiting for something like this to happen." There was a dangerous glint in her eyes as she turned on the hulking outlaw. "Kip's been at you to pull out of here. Now you can break up this precious gang, Helm Spink," she proclaimed, "and send them packing! I'm going home; Indy's going home; and Kip with us . . . And you, Mister Spink, are going too!"

Helm instantly let loose a vehement protest, but his defense was noticeably weak. Under Madge's burning glare he sputtered off into silence.

India and Colerain quickly forgot their spat, the prospect of an early release filling them with animation. "There sure is a lot of work to catch up with back there at Coldwater," the puncher said. From his hopeful air he was eager to be at it.

" 'Break up this gang—send 'em packing!' . . . That's a tall order," Spink groaned to Pat when they stepped outside later. "She simply don't know what she's doin' to me. Dang a bossy woman anyhow!" It was evident as he spoke that he was thoroughly cowed by this one.

"It may be wise advice at that," said Pat mildly. "We're not out of this yet. Once men like these get familiar they don't know where to stop. You can't have them bothering Madge."

Helm nodded gloomy agreement. Strangely enough he meant to abide by Madge's iron mandate no matter what happened; but he refused Pat's offer to help him deal with the outlaws.

"Leave this to me. I'll brace the boys tonight—I won't tell 'em I'm taking the women back to Powder Valley. They'll find it convenient to pull away from the Roost for the time being," he concluded with gathering resolution. "or I'll make it my business to find out why!"

Since his success or failure had much to do with their own safe departure, Pat and the partners were not far away when Spink authoritatively summoned the owlhoots to the bar that evening. The three friends kept out of sight, but they were not long in gathering that the big man was in for a stormy session.

Spink, however, was thoroughly aroused and firm in his purpose. He weathered a clash or two by kicking some noisy objectors bodily from the saloon, and it began presently to appear that he was winning his bitterly contested point. Half-a-dozen muttering outlaws saddled up and pulled out without delay; and in the morning the continuing exodus was general as the homeless drifters rode out in groups.

Before noon Kip Colerain was able to report that the Roost was virtually abandoned. Even Trap Hagen had taken his cue and pulled out alone. Spink met Pat and his friends in dour triumph as they approached the hotel.

"Get your traps packed," he instructed curtly. "The boss says we're headin' out directly after dinner, and I ain't anxious myself to give those boys time to think things over." He eyed them all severely. "Don't know as there's much I can add to that. It's a long haul back to Powder Valley—and since I won't have any peace to speak of till we land them women in their own dooryard, we might as well get about it!"

19.

AN OMINOUS SILENCE lay over Robber's Roost as the little party headed the horses toward Green River for the last time. Spink, leading the way with Madge Pickett near at hand, sat his saddle with a somber face. He had little to say.

Colerain and India were far more animated, however. They chattered together, looking at everything about them with keen interest now that they were leaving it all behind. But for the rest there was no false cheer over the start for home. None knew what lay ahead except rigorous travel. They would be traversing outlaw country for several days at least, and Pat did not for an instant suppose they would be allowed to pass unmolested.

He guessed right. That night, as they were camping in the lower canyon a mile from Green River gorge, they heard clattering horses pass swiftly down the rocky trail. No one entered the sheltered branch canyon into which they had turned. But clearly the dispersed owlhoots were gathering for no good purpose.

They thrust on next morning in a close group, doubly watchful now but meeting with no overt opposition until, well past the ford, they were climbing the red sandstone benches that led up to the high Colorado back range. Here, at a narrow notch between the ridges, a delegation of dour-faced outlaws awaited them.

Halting his party, Spink gazed speculatively up the ragged sage slope. "Reckon I know them boys. Hold the rest here," he ordered Pat, "while I talk to 'em."

With a severe look on her hard-bitten face Madge opened her mouth to speak, then closed it. She watched as the big man jogged straight forward; and for five minutes the tiny figures at the notch held a heated conference. Then came the flat crack of a shot! Spink tried to ride down a man as the riders scattered, and faint yells broke the silence. Left alone at the notch, Helm presently waved his party forward.

The small group drilled on, passing unhindered through this lonely gap. Their big leader professed contempt for the poorly organized opposition he had succeeded in breaking up, but his lookout sharpened. Asked by Sam Sloan who was behind this work, Spink snorted.

"Pack of stupid fools—still mad because I broke up the Roost!"

Colerain was instantly up in arms, alert at any threat to India's escape. "You bluffed through that time. What if we should run into Gentry and the tag end of his crowd all primed for trouble?" he demanded.

Helm only shrugged, and it was crusty Ezra who replied. "Treat him to his own medicine," he spoke up flatly. But all realized that if they did meet the tricky renegade it would be in a deadlier ambush than any they had yet seen.

There were signs during the afternoon that they were being persistently trailed. Riders were glimpsed in the distance, but none ventured to plant themselves in the path of the traveling party. They pitched camp that night under a rocky overhang and set a close guard. The night dragged by without incident, and before dawn the following morning they were well on their way.

Two hours later a rifle cracked from a flat-crowned butte overlooking their course. The slug flew wild, and when Pat ruled against any active retaliation they spurred the horses on, soon drawing beyond range. Thereafter for two days they were similarly harassed at odd times and from unexpected quarters, though without serious consequences beyond a punctured frying pan. It was not till the broken ranges of the Rockies lay behind that they felt the incensed inmates of Robber's Roost had given up their feud and drawn off.

MAN FROM ROBBER'S ROOST

They breathed easier climbing the pine-blackened slopes of the Isabels, with only the rugged Culebras lying between them and Powder Valley. The young couple was almost exuberant, and even Madge relaxed somewhat her rigorous watch over the group's activities. She also showed signs of slackening her iron command over Spink, deferring to his judgment so markedly that Sam and Ezra grinned and the big man shook his head in frank puzzlement. "I dunno. Sometimes the old girl acts almost human," he muttered to Pat.

The latter smiled faintly. "If you think we've got things licked—or she thinks so—don't let it fool you," he warned. "Not all our troubles are behind us. They could be just starting."

Helm chewed over the thought fretfully, without slackening his pace. He seemed bent on depositing the women quickly and safely at Coldwater Canyon. Perhaps he hoped his responsibility would end there.

He could scarcely have been further from the truth. On a day which looked as if the prolonged streak of fine weather would finally break, Helm led the way triumphantly down the final slopes of the Culebras and onto Spade range. Madge gazed about her complacently but sharply. There were the grazing Circle C Bar steers, obviously in good condition.

"You'll soon be steppin' into your own house," Spink told India with satisfaction.

"That will seem wonderful," she breathed, her eyes seeking Kip's.

Riding up to the little log ranch house on the bench, they all dismounted with weary pleasure and went inside at Madge's brief announcement that hot coffee would be ready directly. They were gathered there discussing the long trip from the Roost and vaguely prospecting a future free of the attentions of Lant Palmer when there was a peremptory rap at the door. Ezra swung it back to disclose Jess Lawlor, the rugged Powder County sheriff, standing on the steps.

"Got here, did you?" The lawman's heavy glance traveled over them. "I heard you were on your way—"

For a second there was silence as they stared at him. "Glad to hear you've interested yourself in us, Lawlor," Pat spoke up at last. "Any special reason for that?"

"There sure is. Word has got to me, Stevens, that half of Lant Palmer's gang from Robber's Roost is plannin' to raid Powder Valley. I aim to break that up fast!"

With upraised hand Pat silenced the exclamation of resentment and incredulity from Spink and his friends. He turned back. "Where did you pick up that crazy rumor, Lawlor?"

The sheriff's leathery face darkened. "Oh, I hear things—"

"I'll say! And are we supposed to be—a part of this outlaw invasion?"

"Well, Spink's a stranger to this range, if you ain't. And I understand young Colerain was their spy—drifting in here as an innocent puncher to look things over!"

"So you believe that of him, do you? . . . What'll you do with Kip, Sheriff?"

"Arrest him, of course."

"Hold on there, mister," Madge Pickett, who had been stunned by surprise until this moment, barged forward to confront Lawlor. "Just where did you get all this stuff?" she demanded shrewdly. "You never dreamed it up—"

"No matter. Step out here, Spink—you too, boy." Jess's stern eye fastened on the pair. "I'll take you to Dutch Springs and let the Judge iron this out!"

"You and who else?" Madge retorted contemptuously, peering past his brawny frame into the yard. Suddenly the others saw her stiffen. "Is that Jack Gentry out there? *What's he doing on my ranch?*"

Pat Stevens had his own startled look. Rufe Dade and Gentry were lounging in their saddles, self-assured and watchful.

"My deputies, ma'am." Lawlor's tone was stern. "I'll have to order 'em to take charge of these men—"

He got no further. Madge gave him a violent shove that sent him staggering backward. "Get yourself *and* your crumby deputies off my land, fast as the Lord'll let you," her voice rang out. "You and your outlaw gang and your spies and I don't know what not! I'll have you know I'm a respectable rancher. These boys are my ranch hands and my friends. Lay a finger on one of 'em, Mister Law, and see where you wind up!"

Lawlor never had tangled with a woman precisely like her. He argued heatedly, but her stubborn defiance put him at a distinct loss. He withdrew finally to confer with Gentry and Dade, making his displeasure plain.

"Don't think for a minute you can get away with this," he burst out, his irritation advertising temporary defeat. "I refuse to risk bloodshed here, but you can laugh just so long at the law! You'll find yourself talkin' to me again!" When they made no remark he presently drew off with his resentful deputies, despite Gentry's unguarded arguments in favor of using force.

Madge was furious. "Why, that no-good bluffer!" she shouted. "Sheriff, is he? Stupid enough to let Gentry talk him into a bowknot—and then he tries to arrest Helm and Kip!" Her snort was explosive. "We'll just see how far he gets with that!"

Pat approached the dubious situation more soberly. "I never expected Gentry to turn up here, but it looks bad. Jack's gall gets him farther than another man would dare dream of." He was thinking hard. "It will hardly make sense now for Spink and Colerain to risk staying here at Spade. You'll be wide open for trouble," he told the pair plainly.

"I won't leave India alone!" Kip cried in alarm. "With Gentry loose around here? . . . Damn the slimy rattler, I'll ride him down and smash his ugly, lying face!"

"No you won't," ruled Pat promptly. "Lawlor's a blind fool; but with him around nothing can happen to these women. You and Helm are coming with us to the Lazy Mare. A setup like this can't hang fire long. I've a hunch it'll break quick, and I want you two where I can lay hands on you."

After heated discussion the pair grudgingly assented. They were setting out for Pat's ranch when Eph Sample and Candy Evans rode in. Their report on the little spread they had been left to guard was good. Warning them to keep an ever sharper watch for the next few days, Pat left.

No unusual event marked their arrival at the Lazy Mare. At this advanced season on the verge of threatening winter, most of the range work was done. Stevens advised Spink and Kip to stick close to the ranch. Sam and Ezra, however, rode home to the Bar ES to look after private affairs. They were to stop in Dutch Springs on the way and planned to return the next day with any news they had picked up in town.

"Yuh wouldn't believe Gentry's got such a smooth line," declared Sloan the following morning, relating his discoveries in Pat's kitchen. "He's made himself right at home here in the Valley. Can't help wonderin' what Ab Keeler and Winters find to talk t' him about . . . No, I didn't see much of Lawlor," he responded in answer to Stevens's question.

"Plannin' his big campaign, most likely," offered Ezra sagely. "He could be buildin' a posse big enough to suit even Gentry—and then all of us better watch out."

"Something's sure to turn up fast," Pat seconded. "Safe as he seems here, Jack must know he's not long for this range. If Lawlor brings in a U.S. marshal that owlhoot's done for. He'll make his play," he predicted shrewdly, "before anything like that happens."

They discussed the situation pro and con, with Colerain making plain his concern for the girl and her mother. "India Pickett has been Gentry's sole object from the first," he reminded. "I was a fool for allowing you to drag me over here at all, Stevens! Right there on Spade is where I belong—and I think I'm going back!"

It was the old problem of calming the puncher. Pat was just about to reply when a clatter of hoofs outside caused Sam to glance through the window into the yard.

"Some kid," he announced. "Acts like he was packin' news hot off the griddle—"

A ragged, freckled youngster of twelve hammered at the door and burst in. "Are yuh here, Mr. Stevens—?" His glance raked them all, and the Lazy Mare owner spoke up sharply.

"I'm Stevens. What is it, son?"

"Miz Pickett sent me! You're to come runnin'," the

youngster blurted breathlessly. "Indy's disappeared this mornin' and her ma's wild about it—"

For the minute the stupefying announcement left them speechless. Then at Colerain's savage cry they burst into violent action. Helm was in a towering rage. "I thought it would end like this! Get them broncs out of the pen!" He stamped out into the yard. "By grab—no more waitin'! We'll look into this, and then I'll act according!"

They jumped astride their mounts, and with Colerain in the lead struck out for Coldwater Canyon. It was some time before Spink started to glance about.

"Where's Stevens?" he barked.

"He didn't come," Sloan tossed back laconically. "Said for me and Ez to shove along—he wanted to talk some more to that boy."

"Lot o' good that'll do!" Helm scowled without slackening his killing pace. "*I* want to talk to Gentry if he's behind this rotten deal!"

Little more was said as they put the miles behind them. Presently the foothills loomed, and the rocky mouth of Coldwater Canyon opened out. They saw the Pickett ranch house on its flat and raced wildly into the yard. Kip leaped from his running horse and stumbled toward the door.

It opened before he could reach it, revealing India, her eyes wide. "What's wrong, Kip?" she called anxiously. "Has something happened?"

The young fellow almost wilted in relief. "Great cripes!" he groaned. "Then you're all right after all! That little punk lied to us!"

After the first incredulous jolt Spink took the situation more calmly. But he was serious as he explained what had brought them on the run. "Yuh ain't had no trouble here, girl? You've been here all morning—and didn't send no message—?"

"Of course not," said India decidedly. "Why do you insist on that point?" But she was quick to get his thought. "Why, it does look strange—that boy coming to you in just that way! But what does it mean?"

The circumstances looked decidedly ominous. Ezra was the first to make up his mind. "Whatever the rest of yuh do," he asserted flatly, "I'm gettin' back to the Lazy Mare faster'n I came!"

"I'll go with you, of course," India quickly decided. "Mother's somewhere out on the range, and I won't stay alone after this."

Spink's protest died in his throat at the look of relief on Kip's drawn face. "Get her up a pony, boy! We're movin'."

Though silent and uneasy they made good time on the way back. At first glance the Lazy Mare was as peaceful as ever. Crusty Hodge stumped out on the porch at Sam's hail, wizened face a thundercloud.

"Whyn't yuh stay away?" he snarled irascibly. "Yuh was gone when yuh was needed!"

Ezra never wasted patience on this old hardshell, whom he considered useless save for a fierce loyalty to Stevens. "Tell your tale, Hodge!" he commanded.

"It's soon told! Soon as yuh got away Rufe Dade and that smooth talkin' new deputy rode in here. They 'arrested' Stevens, and I expect by now he's been clapped in jail," Crusty tossed his bombshell with a perverse pleasure.

"New deputy . . . That must be Jack Gentry!" India was bewildered. "Why in the world could they have arrested Pat?"

"That's what we'll soon find out," Spink rumbled. "If Stevens is in Dutch Springs we'll soon find him—and we'll learn why at the same time."

They pushed over the trail to town without sparing themselves or the horses, and there was no discussion of the risk they might run in appearing there. "I'd almost be willin' to turn back for Madge," Helm grumbled. "Lawlor don't savvy her very well—but maybe he'll listen to me!"

The little cow town lay somnolent in midafternoon sunshine. Only a few men were about. Spink would have made directly for the sheriff's office, but Sam and Ezra counseled delay while a few discreet inquiries were made. The others waited impatiently while Sloan stepped across the street to accost a man on Jeb Winters's store porch. The pair conversed so long in low tones that Helm began to fidget. Abruptly then, Sam hurried back to them.

"It's worse'n I thought," he reported in a swift undertone. "That pair nabbed Stevens all right, and he's been shoved into a cell down at the jail. Lawlor slapped him with a list of charges as long as your arm: conspiracy to obstruct and defraud the law; consortin' with known outlaws; and taking charge of the Spade ranch by force, with illegal intent to grab the range!"

They could only stare at him thunderstruck.

"That's Gentry's work!" cried Kip. "He's never let up trying to smash us. As Lawlor's deputy he's getting in his licks at last!"

20.

SAM AND EZRA FOUND IT all they could do to stop Helm Spink from storming down to the jail at once. The big man's anger was ferocious. There was a bare vestige of truth in the grave charges leveled against Pat, which made his dilemma all the more ominous. Nevertheless the partners advised delay.

"By gum, I ain't lettin' Stevens sweat this out," the brawny giant swore. "Let Lawlor grab me if he thinks he's able. I'm the one he wants!"

"There's where you're dead wrong," refuted Sam. "Don't be underratin' that boy Pat. Yuh don't suppose he let himself be picked up unless he wanted it that way?"

This was a new slant, and one that gave Helm pause. Yet he was dubious. "Nothing I ever seen of that stout hombre says he's anxious to be tossed in the can—"

"You only think you know him." Ezra grinned. "He's figured out a way to tear down Gentry fast, and that's what he's about now. I'll bet on it."

Spink allowed himself to be persuaded against his will. In the discussion which followed he agreed to lay low overnight. Ezra and Sam planned a conference with Stevens at the jail in the morning, but they absolutely refused to rush matters.

The tall tracker took India to Jeb Winters's home on the edge of town, where the merchant's wife insisted on putting her up for the night. Helm and Kip retired to the barn. The girl had left a note for her mother at Spade, and shortly after ten o'clock Madge came rattling into Dutch

MAN FROM ROBBER'S ROOST 163

Springs in the buckboard. Sam intercepted the woman as she barged into the hotel, fire in her eye.

"Where's that girl of mine?" she demanded. "Has Gentry got a thing to do with this?"

After hastily acquainting her with events Sam succeeded in calming her down only by repeating his conviction that Pat's arrest was undoubtedly a part of the latter's plan to trip up the renegade deputy. Madge snorted impatiently at such doings, but she listened to reason, deciding to remain at the hotel and go to India in the morning.

The Bar ES partners were on hand shortly after daylight the following morning when Rufe Dade unlocked the jail to take Stevens his breakfast. He glared sourly at the pair. "Lookin' for a cell of your own?" he growled in his surly way.

"Get that door open, Dade—and shut your trap," retorted Sam sharply. "If Judge Jeff says we can have our talk with Stevens, that ought t' be good enough for you!"

This was pure bluff. Sloan had been nowhere near Judge Blaine. But mere mention of the dread jurist, who was justly called Ironface on this range, was more than enough for Rufe. "Get it over fast then," he muttered, throwing open the cell block and hovering about till Ezra's cold glare drove him sullenly away.

"Well, Stevens. Growin' weak-minded in your old age?" Sam stuck his pudgy nose through the bars. "Or is it only your back—"

"I've been wondering how long it would take you two to wake up," Pat insulted. His sharp eye raked the corridor. "Where's Gentry right now? Is he out there—?"

"Unh-uh." Sam smirked. "Reckon he's struttin' around town with his chest out. Made a fine jackass out of you, didn't he?"

Pat curtly put an end to the banter by demanding news. While Ezra stood watch, Sam quickly informed him how matters stood. "Spink's all for hauling you out of here pronto," he concluded. "Dunno how long we can hold him off—"

Pat shook his head, frowning. "I don't want anything like that—yet. Turn Madge loose on him," he advised. "She'll slow him down to a walk." Sam appeared to agree, but his curiosity was strong as they talked the matter over in low tones.

"What's your game, boy?" he asked finally. "Time's wastin'—and that girl's just so much bait right here in town with Gentry. You must have some move figured out if you aim to bring him up short."

Pat had done much thinking overnight and his answer was calmy assured. "I want you," he instructed, "to persuade India Pickett that the best thing she can do is to marry young Colerain right off. Today, I mean. This morning if possible—but the quicker the better. Have you got that?"

Sam eyed him incredulously. "Are you bats?" he muttered, obviously dispeased with any such inane plan.

"Never mind! Do as I say." Pat was forced to display considerable firmness before the stocky man reluctantly agreed to do his bidding.

"I'll talk to her," he growled. "It may make more sense t' her than it does to me." His tone said, however, that he thought it unlikely.

He and Ezra left a few moments later, shouldering past Jack Gentry in the door as they stepped out to the street. The brazen renegade glowered at them suspiciously, but he could not disguise the triumph in his eyes.

"You two are lucky to be coming out of there," he sneered. "I just haven't got around to your case yet!"

"No hurry, Gentry," Ezra retorted caustically. "We'll be waitin' when you're ready."

As it turned out, Sam did not go to India after all with Pat's urgent message. Kip Colerain had been out early in the morning and he had trailed Gentry jealously to the jail. He immediately fastened on the partners, demanding word of Stevens. Sloan lost little time in telling him of Pat's proposal that he and the girl should marry at once. "How about that, boy? Maybe you can persuade her. I ain't much of a talker myself," Sam fibbed blandly.

Kip was astonished. "Get married—today? *India and me?* . . . Cripes, Sam! I don't know." Dismay and hope seized him at the idea. "Do you think she'll say yes?" he implored, making plain his own sentiments.

"How in hell do I know?" Sam pretended irritation.

MAN FROM ROBBER'S ROOST 165

"You can ask her, can't you? What are you waitin' for? Get about it and don't be botherin' me with foolish questions!"

A victim of mingled delight and torment, Kip started away on the double, only to circle back. "Hang it! India's mother'll be with her now," he wailed. "How will I ever face her, Sam?" He was plainly fearful of Madge's verdict.

Ezra gave an angry roar. "Yuh want that fine girl, don't yuh? Then don't be askin' us how to work it!" he bellowed. "Figure it out for yourself and don't pester us no more." He smothered a grin as Colerain hurried away.

The pair waited uneasily, asking themselves if they had shirked a vital task in delegating this proposal of marriage to a halfhearted boy; but as matters turned out it was the best thing they could have done. Kip appeared beaming an hour later with the astounding news that all was arranged.

Madge Pickett had unexpectedly bolstered his suit; and India, apparently eager despite her surface hesitations, had finally consented. As a concession to the feminine penchant for delay the girl had pleaded for an afternoon wedding. Madge had clinched it by insisting on a ceremony at the hotel immediately after dinner, and she was already busy making the arrangements.

"Cripes!" Sam grumbled his profound relief to Ez as they went in search of Spink. "That settles that. Stevens has us doin' a lot of fool things, but at least he won't have me playin' cupid this time!"

Pat had warned particularly against allowing plans for the wedding to become public. If he wanted the news to reach Gentry indirectly he did not say so, but it would have been impossible to keep the renegade in ignorance for very long. As the time dragged along toward noon it became increasingly clear that something unusual was afoot at the hotel. Madge was bustling importantly about; India had been transferred to her room upstairs; and the circuit rider who had been commandeered for the occasion was much in evidence.

Spink gruffly claimed he didn't know how much bearing all this fuss and feathers about a wedding was supposed to have on Pat's predicament. He was still all for springing

Stevens without further ado. Zeke Johnson, who rode into Dutch Springs during the morning, flatly refused to have anything to do with the matter; and the foreman's attitude impressed Helm. Madge's firm persuasion settled it, although Spink was anxious to make an end of the affair.

He appeared at the hotel directly after the noon meal and was edging into the parlor, in some doubt as to what to do with his hat and his big hands, when Jess Lawlor confronted him.

"Outside, you." The lawman had been invited by Madge in an unwary moment to keep order and now he officiously constituted himself his own judge of what that duty was. "I won't bother with you now—but no range tramps allowed in here today. Take your troubles across to the bar."

Spink argued to no avail. Lawlor thrust him to the door when his protests threatened to create a disturbance. Helm looked about desperately. He did not understand this business. Rufe Dade grinned at him sardonically from across the room, but Madge, who would have summarily rescued him, was nowhere in sight.

"You're makin' a mistake, Lawlor!" Helm said in disgust. "It's you that'll be sorry for it—so what am I worryin' about?" Whirling, he barged indignantly out of the hotel. "I've had more than enough of this," he muttered. "Whatever Stevens will have t' say, it better be good!"

Although India's marriage to Kip was in progress while he stalked huffily toward the jail he was indifferent to it, brooding over his offended loyalty. It did not strike him as strange that he saw no sign of Jack Gentry, for Spink knew that the shifty renegade, deputy or no, valued his skin.

Pat was first aware of Helm's presence at the jail when he heard a resounding metallic screech as the other man wrenched the gate of the cell block from its fastenings with a confiscated crowbar.

"Who is that? . . . Oh—you?" Pat peered at Helm, not particularly surprised. His voice sharpened. "Is Kip married, Spink, or isn't he?"

"Stand back," the big man ordered tersely. He attacked Pat's cell in businesslike fashion. No steel frame could

MAN FROM ROBBER'S ROOST   167

hope to withstand his tremendous strength when he had the proper leverage. The cell door whined in protest as it bent, then finally snapped open. Pat stepped into the corridor.

"Okay, you've got me out. What about Kip?" He was curt as he accepted the six-gun proffered by Spink.

"Hitched tight, I expect," was Helm's response. Suddenly he froze as the muted clap of gunfire broke the silence. *"What was that?"* he bristled fiercely. "Don't tell me they spotted this two-bit jailbreak already!"

Their answer came shortly, as they heard boots slapping into the jail office and a harsh cry boomed into the corridor. "Stevens! Are yuh there?" It was Sam Sloan and Ezra, filled with excitement.

"What is it, Sam? A siege—?"

"Hell, no! There's a big raid comin' off at Keeler's bank!" Sam announced savagely. "This is Gentry's work, boy! He's sneaked his gang in town, and they're makin' hay while everybody's up at the hotel watchin' Kip get spliced!"

When he heard this, Pat was thankful that Helm had dragged him unceremoniously to freedom. The big man had been none too soon. "Let's go!" Pat was already halfway to the door. "I'm taking a hand in that!"

They raced into the street and headed down toward the bank. Several townsmen were crouched behind wagons and building corners briskly firing into the bank at the bandits.

A hundred yards from the place Stevens dived into a rutted lane turning off the street. Spink would have plunged on past, but he hesitated. "Where yuh goin'?" he panted.

"Come on," Pat called. "Straight through the livery into the alley behind the bank! We could be too late now!"

The four ran through the barn and darted over the cross street below the bank corner. They could see the place now. Glass jingled as the gunfire blasted through the windows from inside.

"Shake it up! We'll nail 'em!" Pat cried at the scuttling trio.

They braved whistling slugs to gain the mouth of the alley. Pat felt a sharp tug at his pants leg, and Sloan got a scratched ear. They were only barely in time.

Several men tumbled out the back door of the bank with heavy sacks over their arms, their guns spitting. Gentry was one of them. Although the rest of the men were all known to Spink he saw only his treacherous one-time crony. "Gentry!" he roared. "Face up to your finish, man!"

He fired simultaneously with Sam as Jack whipped his gun around. One of Gentry's confederates dropped with a cry, and his jingling bags pitched to the dirt. Gentry wheeled to dash up the alley.

"He's making for the hotel," Pat shouted. "Corner the rest of those birds while I block that! There could be one or two still in the bank!"

The renegades broke and scattered in different directions, firing at random. While racing after the bogus deputy Pat saw one of the outlaws turn back, cornered, to chop at Ezra with his empty gun. The lanky redhead kicked the man's legs out from under him and batted him unconscious. Pat forgot them, concentrating on his quarry. Gentry pounded through littered backyards, cunningly making use of every obstruction. Twice Pat's shots missed by the narrowest margin. The third time, however, Gentry's left arm wilted and dropped the heavy coin sack, which bounced away.

With a snarl of rage Jack unleashed a fusillade. The lead whined lethally about Pat, though miraculously he was not hit. Wheeling, Gentry dashed for the rear entrance of the hotel. Halting in his tracks, Stevens sternly leveled his Colt for one last try. Crack! Gentry stumbled, almost at the steps. Blood gushed on his thigh. He made the door and plunged through to momentary cover.

The wedding reception was in full swing in the hotel parlor. Surrounded by laughter and talk—and blissfully ignorant of other events—Kip Colerain was dazedly receiving congratulations at India's side. Suddenly a door burst open with a crash. Jack Gentry stood there, bloody and with gleaming eyes.

"Well, Colerain!" The cry knifed through the startled silence. "Looks like I'm slated for a long trip! Here's where I send you ahead of me!"

If he had not raised the gun so deliberately he might

have gained his deadly object. Kip never delayed an instant. Grabbing up one of his and India's few gifts from the table—a heavy china plate bestowed by Mrs. Winters—the puncher hurled it squarely into Gentry's face. His aim was good. The dish exploded in fragments, toppling the renegade over backwards with a jarring crash.

"Good shot, boy!" Pat appeared in the door as Sheriff Lawlor crowded through the guests. "He's out cold. Better work than I did with a chopper!"

"What in creation goes on here?" blazed Lawlor furiously. "I left you in a cell, Stevens—!"

"And you left your deputy in charge of the town," Pat reminded him coolly. "His gang was robbing the bank, Sheriff, while you stood guard over a blameless puncher! I had no choice but to step in."

Lawlor was about to retort with bitter countercharges when Spink ran in, with Sloan close behind him. "Did you grab him, Stevens?"

"Kip stopped him, Helm. Shouldn't wonder if the boy rates a reward for this—"

Lawlor masked his stupefaction as Sloan gave a terse version of the bank holdup. "We nabbed all of Gentry's gang that's still navigatin', and Ab'll get his money back." The stocky man broke off. "How in Hannah did yuh guess that wolf on the floor was headed for here, Stevens?"

Pat smiled. "Easy enough to figure Kip's wedding would drive Gentry off his rocker. Jack was so chesty he'd bluff a bobtailed flush for the pot. He meant to clean the bank, down Colerain, grab India again and run, giving us all the horselaugh." He let this sink in. "He didn't quite make it—thanks to Spink, and Kip, and a few others."

Sheriff Lawlor could be thickheaded on occasion, but he saw clearly enough through a brick wall with a sizable hole in it. He slapped Gentry roughly back to sullen consciousness and hauled him unsteadily to his feet.

"It wasn't no mistake makin' you a deputy so I could keep an eye on you," Jess growled shamelessly.

"Now that's quick thinking," Madge put in candidly. "You won't mind giving my son-in-law and the rest of my menfolks a clean slate, I dare say, while you're about it—"

Lawlor had no desire to clash with her again if he could help it. He knew when he was licked. "Well, I wasn't wrong about them owlhoots from the Roost. Right now I'm interested in grabbin' the leader of Lant Palmer's crowd," he said defensively scowling at Gentry. "I reckon I got him!"

"Oh, Kip!" India threw her arms joyfully about her husband. Her mother, who had no intention of being overlooked, fastened firmly on the lawman's words.

"You couldn't be righter, Mister Sheriff," she announced, turning abruptly to the hulking giant at her side. "From now on, Helm Spink, you're nothing but my husband." She competently ignored the startled gaze of all, resuming crisply: "It's a good thing we got married on our trip to Pueblo, or I'd never consented to go along and look after such a pack of brainless men! From now on I expect to find it a lot easier."

It was obvious from the heavy silence which followed her words, punctuated by a sardonic chuckle from Ezra, that more than one of these men were in hearty agreement with her prediction.

CLASSIC ADVENTURES FROM THE DAYS OF THE OLD WEST FROM AMERICA'S AUTHENTIC STORYTELLERS

NORMAN A. FOX

DEAD END TRAIL	70298-3/$2.75US/$3.75Can
NIGHT PASSAGE	70295-9/$2.75US/$3.75Can
RECKONING AT RIMBOW	70297-5/$2.75US/$3.75Can
TALL MAN RIDING	70294-0/$2.75US/$3.75Can
STRANGER FROM ARIZONA	70296-7/$2.75US/$3.75Can
THE TREMBLING HILLS	70299-1/$2.75US/$3.75 Can

LAURAN PAINE

SKYE	70186-3/$2.75US/$3.75Can
THE MARSHAL	70187-1/$2.50US/$3.50Can
THE HOMESTEADERS	70185-5/$2.75US/$3.75Can

T.V. OLSEN

BREAK THE YOUNG LAND	75290-5/$2.75US/$3.75Can
KENO	75292-1/$2.75US/$3.95Can
THE MAN FROM NOWHERE	75293-X/$2.75US/$3.75Can

Buy these books at your local bookstore or use this coupon for ordering:

Avon Books, Dept BP, Box 767, Rte 2, Dresden, TN 38225
Please send me the book(s) I have checked above. I am enclosing $_____
(please add $1.00 to cover postage and handling for each book ordered to a maximum of three dollars). *Send check or money order*—no cash or C.O.D.'s please. Prices and numbers are subject to change without notice. Please allow six to eight weeks for delivery.

Name _____

Address _____

City _____ State/Zip _____

WES/TRAD 9/88

Please allow 6-8 weeks for delivery

SEALS

THE WORLD'S MOST RUTHLESS FIGHTING UNIT, TAKING THE ART OF WARFARE TO THE LIMIT — AND BEYOND!

SEALS #1: AMBUSH!	75189-5/$2.95US/$3.95Can
SEALS #2: BLACKBIRD	75190-9/$2.50US/$3.50Can
SEALS #3: RESCUE!	75191-7/$2.50US/$3.50Can
SEALS #4: TARGET!	75193-3/$2.95US/$3.95Can
SEALS #5: BREAKOUT!	75194-1/$2.95US/$3.95Can
SEALS #6: DESERT RAID	75195-X/$2.95US/$3.95Can
SEALS #7: RECON	75529-7/$2.95US/$3.95Can
SEALS #8: INFILTRATE!	75530-0/$2.95US/$3.95Can
SEALS #9: ASSAULT!	75532-7/$2.95US/$3.95Can
SEALS #10: SNIPER	75533-5/$2.95US/$3.95Can

and coming soon from Avon Books

SEALS #11: ATTACK!	75582-3/$2.95US/$3.95Can
SEALS #12: STRONGHOLD	75583-1/$2.95US/$3.95Can

Buy these books at your local bookstore or use this coupon for ordering:

Avon Books, Dept BP, Box 767, Rte 2, Dresden, TN 38225
Please send me the book(s) I have checked above. I am enclosing $_____
(please add $1.00 to cover postage and handling for each book ordered to a maximum three dollars). *Send check or money order*—no cash or C.O.D.'s please. Prices and numbers are subject to change without notice. Please allow six to eight weeks for delivery.

Name _____

Address _____

City _____ State/Zip _____

SEALS 11/

HEARTS OF TEXAS

■ ■ ■ ■ ■ ■

KRISTEN NORDSTROM. A passionate golden-haired beauty, she was the coveted prize of both Comanche and Comanchero—and the one woman the Texan would love.

IRON CHEEK. The renowned Comanche chief, he ravaged the land and its people at will, sparing neither white nor Indian.

SALVADOR DE SANTOS. The hot-blooded Comanchero, he traded in horse-flesh, trafficked in human lives and pursued the one woman he could never possess.

KATE NORDSTROM. A true woman of the frontier, she possessed the beauty and sinew that would help build a nation.

FRANK KILRAIN. The Nordstroms' ranch foreman, he burned with a grudge that would one day explode in fiery revenge against...

THE TEXAN

ATTENTION: SCHOOLS AND CORPORATIONS

POPULAR LIBRARY books are available at quantity discounts with bulk purchase for educational, business, or sales promotional use. For information, please write to SPECIAL SALES DEPARTMENT, POPULAR LIBRARY, 666 FIFTH AVENUE, NEW YORK, N Y 10103

**ARE THERE POPULAR LIBRARY BOOKS
YOU WANT BUT CANNOT FIND IN YOUR LOCAL STORES?**

You can get any POPULAR LIBRARY title in print. Simply send title and retail price, plus 50¢ per order and 50¢ per copy to cover mailing and handling costs for each book desired. New York State and California residents add applicable sales tax. Enclose check or money order only, no cash please, to POPULAR LIBRARY, P. O. BOX 690, NEW YORK, N Y 10019